THE WOMAN DOCTOR

Anna Thorpe qualified as a doctor at a time when women were new to the job. Believing that she had got a job, she actually took a charming old house in the area only to find that they did not want her after all. Anna had no choice but to set up her plate. This was not a good start, but the best doctors in the town were serving in the First World War, and people were glad to have a new practice starting. But Anna was worried about what would happen when the doctors who were serving in the war returned to the town.

THE WOMAN DOCTOR

URSULA BLOOM

FIRECREST
BATH

First published 1978
by
Hutchinson & Co (Publishers) Ltd
This Large Print edition published by
Firecrest Publishing Limited
Combe Park, Bath
by arrangement with the copyright holder
1979

ISBN 0 85119 039 1

© Ursula Bloom 1978

British Library Cataloguing in Publication Data

Bloom, Ursula
   The woman doctor.—Large print ed.
I. Title
823'.9'1F   PR6003.L58W/

ISBN 0-85119-039-1

Photoset and printed in Great Britain by
Redwood Burn Limited, Trowbridge & Esher
Bound by Cedric Chivers Limited, Bath

THE WOMAN DOCTOR

FOREWORD

As the train approached the small town of Weston, it let out a childish, rather *piano* shriek to attract the attention of the passengers. Anna Thorpe looked out of the window with eager eyes. This could perhaps be the background of her new life, and mean everything to her. She saw a little huddle of a country town with a river on the far side, and hills beyond rising in the dim blue of early hyacinths in spring.

Instantly she realized that on ordinary days the town would be quiet, but on market days it could buzz with excitement and chatter, village and town gossip mixing. The train jerked to a standstill at the dilapidated platform, for in 1918, with the end of a ghastly war in sight, all England was in rags.

Anna had trained at one of the big London hospitals, staying on to become an FRCS, and now she knew that she was stepping out into the world with her first practice in view. It was a time in the history of medicine when women doctors were rare; they were not encouraged (it was a trifle 'unladylike'), but her father had been a GP, fascinating her with stories of his profession, and all that it had meant to him. He had inspired her from the time when she was very small indeed. He had told her how important it was, if surgery interested one, to become a Fellow of the Royal College of Surgeons; he had never allowed himself the time to take it himself, he had had to get on with the good work and earn something. Earning and learning at the same time when you are working for your Fellowship do not go well together.

As she stepped out of the train the porter greeted her almost as an old friend. At that time she did not realize how small towns talk, but he knew that today a 'lady doctor was coming here to see Dr Webb', and he directed her how to find his house.

'You turn right by the fountain, miss, you can't possibly miss that.'

She walked into the amiable September afternoon. Like every other place in England at this time, the town was shabby. Paintwork had peeled away, walls were cracked, and repairs were needed wherever you looked. Four years of war had scarred this country badly, with broken gates, leaking roofs, and windows with holes in them. The town advertised that the wounds of war were not confined to the front.

Anna knew that this was still an era when a woman doctor was considered by some to be rather odd. She supposed that she had inherited her love of medical matters from her dead father; it had been a flame which was constantly rising in her own heart.

Her father had died young, having qualified only ten years before, and she had always wanted to carry on where he had left off. She herself had qualified at his own hospital, and then worked for her Fellowship of the Royal College, which was most unusual at a time when few women even went in for medicine.

Then she had grown tired of the eternal grind of a large hospital, and had decided to break into the routine of a private practice. Perhaps the war had been mainly responsible for this, for once she had thought that she was dedicated to hospital life, but she *had* tired of it. There was the everlasting toll of the maimed and wounded, no home life at all, and the time came when she longed for a private practice. The war had changed everything so enormously; the endless trail of the hopelessly shattered, and the eternal fight with death attacking those who had the right to live for many more years, had made medicine more and more urgent. Death is the last visitor, who never forgets to call, and when he comes it is the end. She had seen too many die.

'War is a horrible thing, and all this waste of life is getting me down,' she told herself.

She had seen the advertisement in a medical paper, from a small country town in Warwickshire, where her father had often stayed as a boy.

Now she walked out of a very ordinary war-shoddied station into a rather smug little town.

She knew that her entire future depended on what happened today, on the interview with two doctors, who admitted to middle age (as indeed most of the doctors left at home had to do).

She saw the hills rising beyond the town, blue, as her father had always said they were, and she got the idea that luck was with her, and this in itself was a thrill. Instinctively she liked the place, even if the war had decayed it almost beyond belief. Tired curtains were frayed at windows. It was the era of the venetian blind, which (unrepaired for four solid years) now hung with dripping slats, providing great holes through which anyone could see the insides of the rooms.

It seemed that the whole of England was war-wounded.

The fountain, of which the porter had appeared to be so proud, was possibly late-Victorian, put there in memory of one of the Queen's Jubilees, no doubt, but now waterless and very dirty. Anna turned right into a quiet street away from the shops, and for the first time caught sight of the doctors' house. It was large and looked comfortable, a typical doctor's residence, with the brass well polished, and on the gate were the names of three doctors, but she knew that the youngest had been killed at the front.

She rang the bell, liked the pleasant echo of it, and whilst waiting outside turned and then saw the old black and white Elizabethan house next door, only a few yards up the street. It had in front of it a rather tired notice-board announcing that it was for sale.

'If I get the job, that would suit me,' she told herself, 'close at hand, and just my era.'

That was when the maid opened the door.

The first impression that she got was of a large hall leading through into an inner one, where an old dresser gleamed with well-polished pewter. She was shown into what was obviously the dining-room, papered in red as was the pre-war mode, and the man who rose from the easy chair by the fire was Dr Webb, the senior partner. He was much older than she had anticipated, close to the eighties, she would have thought, a widower, and inclined to pompousness.

'Do please sit down,' and he had the manner of someone watching her closely, as though wanting to know more of her, even to find fault. She told him that she was not afraid of work, and she did not mind how far she had to drive out into the country to a case. He appreciated that. He had been afraid that she might find him and his partner a trifle old-fashioned, but they did not want any new ways in a long-established practice. They had always stuck to the *old* rules, and they would wish to continue this way.

She now came to the conclusion that he was the dogmatic type, a driver! He explained that he was too old to go far, and his partner found it difficult, so they needed someone to do the 'village jobs' and the places around, while they concentrated more on the small town itself. Two of the local doctors were at the front, a third man had died there. They needed someone who could cope with the distant calls, and there would be operations, which was what she wanted.

He said, 'You'll be all right. You're young, and youth can cope with most things.'

That was when the second doctor, Dr

Higgs, arrived. He was a smally-built man, obviously in the sixties, the over-chatty kind, who go down well with old ladies, but drive men mad! He talked fast. The salary was good (better than she would have anticipated), and, reading between the lines, she gathered that, with so many doctors at the front, they had had some considerable difficulty in getting any response to their enquiries. Dr Higgs tried to be very nice to her.

'I hope you had a good trip down?' he said. 'But today the trains stop everywhere, and take too long.'

'Alas,' said the old man, 'everything has changed. It can never be the same world again.' He blurred his words when speaking, and she wondered if at some time he had had a slight stroke, and this was why they wanted a third partner.

The house had charm, and an excellent tea came in, at a time when excellent teas were few and far between. Dr Webb had been here for forty-five years, and Dr Higgs had been his partner for twenty of those years. He wanted to tell her his story, rather than listen to her, the frequent fault of the very old. She knew they could offer her the future that she wanted, and was pleased with the idea.

'Surgery is your main interest?' he said.

'You took a good degree, of course, but to the ordinary patient the degree is of no consequence. The thing we want is someone to get on with the work.'

She understood this.

'You'll be wanting somewhere to live; there is a most charming house alongside ours, which has been for sale for quite a time. The old lady died, and they have reduced the price to something very favourable. It is fully furnished, all being sold in one, and there is a housekeeper in residence. If you could get that, it would be very useful.'

She asked if he meant the house she had seen when coming in, and which she had liked the look of. It was one that she particularly admired. It was also very close to them, as Dr Webb mentioned, and if she considered coming into the partnership it might be the very thing. It was now plain that they liked the idea of this, though they had not committed themselves. Women doctors were unusual, and might be unacceptable in a small country town, and they would have to discuss this a little further. He did not admit that she had been the only applicant, and they much wanted to get things settled. She liked children, and could take on the maternity side, which always took a lot of time, and a single case of this nature could keep them away for hours.

'But we don't spoil them here!' grunted old Dr Webb in an amused manner, and she did not care too much about this.

She said that she too would think it over, meanwhile she would have a look at the black and white house next door. They seemed to be disappointed that she did not say yes straight away, but obviously the job was in the bag. The pay was good, and even if a woman doctor was rare in this part of the world, she did hold better degrees than they did, which should help her. She left them, certain that the job was hers for the taking.

But she did make her final decision in about half an hour and called again at the surgery to tell Dr Webb that she would like to join the practice, and then she had the inspiration that this was one of the lucky days that come into people's lives, a day when everything went right. She remembered her mother saying that on some days it all went well, and on others the reverse happened. This seemed to be a very lucky twenty-four hours for her.

She visited the house next door, and liked it very much. She felt that it had grown slightly tired, for in the war people were not buying houses, or keeping them in repair. They were waiting 'till the boys come home', and then everyone would be fighting for somewhere to live.

Miss Willis, who opened the door to her, was a woman in her forties, stoutening slightly, but an amiable reliable woman; Anna knew this immediately. She ushered the girl inside. There was an attractive sitting-room looking out on to the garden, and she liked the old-fashioned furniture. Anna took to Miss Willis, who discreetly conveyed that she did not care too much for the doctors next door. Anna felt that her future was falling into her lap. A job and a home which she would adore. Her luck *was* in.

'But I have not yet signed the contract with the doctors,' she said, speaking her thoughts aloud, and she couldn't think of buying the house until she had.

'Oh, they'll want you. They have been looking everywhere for help for ages, and couldn't get anybody,' Miss Willis told her.

It was one of those moments which come in life when one wants to take action. She realized that there had not been so many big opportunities in her life. A delightful home would be a real joy. Everything seemed to be dropping into her lap. Her mother had always said, 'When chance offers something, grab it, for it may never come again,' and she had believed this to be the right thing to do.

So she went along and signed for the house, because it enchanted her, and the idea of owning it herself was an inspiration. The fact that it was ready furnished charmed her, and, after all, there was no need for her to cling to her small capital now that she was getting a good job, and she needed a home of her own.

This was certainly a moment in life when one does take action. A thrilling moment had led her on. She knew from Miss Willis that the old man had been looking for a partner for ages, she knew also that she wanted this house tremendously, and that she had just enough money to pay for it.

If she waited until the war ended (though that end did seem to be almost in sight), she felt that with all the men returning, and the doctors too, houses would be certain to go up in price, and the demand for them would be terrific. This was the right moment to take action, so she went along to the agent's office, she had just sufficient time, and she settled it then and there.

She felt elated.

They had got rather tired of the black and white house on their books, so she gathered, for it had been on their list for quite a time now, dropping in price all the while. She wrote out a cheque to secure it straight away, and she thoroughly enjoyed signing it, for there are times when suddenly an outside influence seems to take control. There was a surveyor's report which someone else had had, it seemed to be entirely satisfactory, and it delighted her. In everybody's life there comes the chance moment when a door appears to open on the future, and she felt that on the instant the whole world had changed for her. It was a glowing moment.

She had a sense of exuberance as she signed the cheque. It might not have been the way a man would have bought himself a house (and she *had* rushed it), but the impulse gave her a delicious thrill. 'Everything is in my lap,' she told herself. Within a few hours she had taken a deliberate step into the future, one which a short time back she would never have dreamed of taking.

'It is awfully nice sometimes to go mad,' she told herself as she made a dash to catch her train.

When she got back to hospital—and the train was very late—a doctor friend to whom she talked about it all, an older man, said, 'You did the right thing in grabbing that house when you could. With the war ending, and the men returning, every spare house in England will be snapped up, and even then there will be insufficient to go round. The doctors will flood back wanting jobs, and houses to go with them.'

'I got it furnished, too, *with* a housekeeper!'

'You did the right thing. I'd say the old doctor will die fairly soon, and you will probably get some of his patients.'

The idea had struck her, but she hated the thought of stepping into a dead man's shoes, and said so. The older man was perhaps the more difficult of the two, and miles behind the times. The problem of the out-of-date partner is tricky in medicine, and no one dies to order. But it had been a most tremendous day's work. She had actually bought this most charming house, and so close, with a housekeeper, and everything to hand.

The house agents acted extremely quickly, as she had asked them to do. She would never have thought that she could get so much done in such a short afternoon, but she *had* done it. It was after eleven when she was back in her digs, and she was triumphant at having done so well.

The doctors had promised to write immediately to confirm the offer, but three days passed and no letter came. This worried her, though she felt quite sure that everything was all right. But she wanted to get her plans finally settled before the war ended, and it was now in its last stages. She must get everything in writing.

She waited another twenty-four hours, and then became agitated. She had secured the lovely new home, and with it Miss Willis, who was a host in herself, and she knew she would be an enormous help to her. She was prepared to sign, as she had conveyed to the doctors at the time, though she would be expected to do the long-distance jobs, but this she did not mind. Neither of them was good with cars, in fact the old man had had trouble with his engine, which had, as he said, put him off.

Still no letter arrived, and, becoming dismayed, she wondered more and more if she *had* rushed it. Everything had gone so well, almost too well, and she asked herself if she had been silly.

Two days later, she rang up and got the old doctor on the other end. She told him that no letter had come, and as she had bought the adjacent house, as they had suggested, she was a trifle worried that she had not heard anything. He could not understand why no letter had arrived, for he said that they had written to her the next day. He and his partner had had a very long talk about it after she had gone, and in the end they had come to the conclusion that a woman doctor would not be desirable in this country neighbourhood. It was an old-time practice, in a very old-fashioned behind-the-times part of the world.

As she listened, it seemed that a cold horror vibrated through her. In their conversation they had given only the slightest hint of this, and when she had originally applied they had known that she was a woman. It was as if her own sex fought her. During the interview they had been a trifle vague, but pleased with her, had suggested the house, and had never mentioned that they did not want a woman doctor there.

She had been so sure that the job was hers, especially when they had told her of the house next door, which she had now bought. She certainly could not go back on that arrangement. She recalled that it had been up for sale for some considerable time, which meant that selling it again would not be easy. She could not afford to lose by it. There was now nothing that she could do save commit the heinous sin of putting up her plate next door to the surgery of the other two doctors.

'To think that I shall have to descend to

this!' she said to herself with some shock. It was something that no decent doctor would ever choose to do, but what else was possible? And why had they changed their minds? They had given her every impression of being glad that she had applied, and would be quite pleased to have her with them.

By the look of both the men, one about sixty, and the other near eighty, she would have thought, they were ageing badly, and out of date with modern medicine.

'What on earth do I do?' she asked herself, with dismay in her heart. It was a ghastly situation.

There were two other doctors in the town at the moment, for Miss Willis had told her this. A Dr Brown who drank heavily, so that nobody had him if they could help it, and old Dr Jackson, who had worked himself to death going everywhere on a bicycle, and was known as 'the poor man's doctor'. He would be retiring soon.

She realized that no small town had ever needed a good doctor more than Weston did, and surely the fact that she had her FRCS would be something of a help? Either she took the bit between her teeth, went down there, and did put up her plate, or she tried to sell the house she had bought, and started all over again.

Within the month she had put up her plate.

On that first afternoon she had been so sure that the two men wanted her and liked her, and that her FRCS would be of help to them. She wondered if they had been jealous of it. What she did not know at the time (but later Miss Willis discovered it, she was always first with the news) was that Dr Webb's nephew, a dolt of a lad, who until now had failed in his examinations, had suddenly passed, and he would come to them for half the salary that Anna was offered. And they also felt that the nephew, being male, would probably be more popular.

They were mean old men who had privately disliked the thought of a woman doctor, and *were* a trifle jealous of her degree. This was the truth.

Anna set up her plate, and she prayed that some day, some time, somehow, a patient would come to her. What she would do if no one turned up, she could not think, she had just sufficient money to last out until Christmas, and after that—what? Easter, she told herself sadly, might see her own post mortem.

Miss Willis was inspiringly hopeful, for she said a good doctor was what this town wanted, and since the war, when the two really good men had joined up, had never had.

'The patients will come all right,' she told Anna. 'This town is sick to death of doddering old doctors, and they'll come if only to see what a lady doctor looks like!'

She happened to be absolutely right.

CHAPTER ONE

In some ways, although she did not recognize this at first, Anna was fortunate, though during her opening week she could not sleep at night, but lay awake praying for the telephone to ring, and thinking that she must have been mad to commit herself to this.

There was a very nasty accident at the street corner, and she was called out to it. She went as she was, and herself took the man with a broken leg to hospital. When she got there she felt that the nurses were cool to her, and she adopted what she called her 'operation theatre manner' and made them do their work for her. When she had done, Matron—a most pleasant woman—asked her into her own private room, where she had some tea ready for her, and for this Anna was truly grateful.

Matron was a large amiable woman, who had been here even before the war started, and she was only too glad to welcome new blood to the place, also having the greatest respect for Anna's degree. Matron (a born chatterbox, which does not go too well with the job) said that the small town and the hospital itself had had many troubles in the war. The two good men had gone, and here they were left, like many other such places, with just what they could get. The consultants were overtired with doing too much work. As to the two old doctors living next door to her, they should have retired years ago. They were bored with the eternal work that the medical world demanded, and, with a war on they were doing too many people's jobs. Matron and the hospital had suffered badly with the best consultants at the front, and the old men sick of their work, and only waiting to retire.

Anna and the matron took to each other on sight, even though they were as the poles apart in temperament. Matron approved of the way Anna had worked, and liked the idea of having someone of her own sex to whom she could turn. She said that the war had lasted far too long, and everybody was tired out as a result of it.

In a way this was one of Anna's lucky days, for when she got back home there was a hectic telephone message about a baby suffering from convulsions. It was a local solicitor's first child, the nanny on holiday, and the wife did not know what to do about it. Anna went straight round.

The ten-month-old child was teething, and she got him through and back into his cot, warning the anxious mother that he could have another attack. At this the distraught mother broke down.

'He'll die,' she sobbed, 'and I've been told that I can't have another.'

'No, he won't! He'll be all right,' Anna insisted, and tried to cheer the poor thing up. 'Lots of babies have convulsions when teething. Stay with him, as he *could* have another one. It's that double tooth of his that's doing it; he has got frightened over it,' and then she looked at the weeping girl. 'And don't be so certain that you can never have another baby. We'll go into that a bit later on. For now, hot water is the answer for this one, but be sure it is not too hot, for mothers get worried and do the wrong thing, and that can be really awful.'

Anna comforted the woman—in her early twenties—and she left her in a far better mood. She was to ring up if there was any sign of another attack, and Anna would come round at once. 'Immediately,' she said, and she meant it.

She felt that tonight she had done rather well. These were the foundation stones of her practice, she supposed, everyone who puts up a plate has to lay them. Next morning she got a call out into the countryside to a farm in the hills. She went to it. She admitted that the instructions which the woman gave her were a bit vague; her last one had been, 'When the road leaves off in a field, you just come on. You can see our farm some yards on ahead, sunk down in a dip, but the chimneys show.'

It all seemed rather different from district visiting in London, from one slum residence to the next, and instructions from the hospital itself—Don't-hang- up-a-coat- any-where-or- you'll-be-all-over-fleas-and-bugs! which was such a charming thought.

The little farm was scrupulously clean, no fear in hanging up your coat here, and it was run by a woman in her forties, and her slightly older husband. It was her old father who was the thorn in the flesh, for he was slowly—too slowly—dying. The woman opened the door to her, tired-looking and obviously overworked.

She said, 'Oh, my goodness, a lady! And I wanted the new doctor.'

'I *am* the new doctor, and I hope I have come to help you.' She smiled as she walked inside.

The woman, who looked at the end of her tether, began to cry. 'It's me dad,' she said.

'He'll never get no better, I know that, and it may be months yet afore he goes. Me 'usband gets fed up and shouts at 'im, and then I gets mad with 'im. There's ever such a lot to do making the farm work, and the old man takes a lot of time and seeing after. He don't seem to know 'e's working me to death.'

Anna nodded. 'And there is no local home into which he could go?'

'Oh no, 'e wouldn't never do that, I couldn't let 'im go neither, for the neighbours would talk.' By the view from the window, the nearest neighbours seemed to be some miles off, and Anna thought that rather a silly excuse.

She said, 'Let me have a look at him.'

The woman's diagnosis had been fairly accurate, but he had a heart murmur which might hasten things. Undoubtedly he would never get any better, but there was nothing to kill him, unless providence intervened, and in her own experience providence was never a great help. She made out a prescription for him and then talked to the woman.

She said, 'Look here, I'm going to try to find a good home for him, there must be somewhere. You can't keep going on this way, whatever the neighbours say, you are doing too much, and then your husband gets annoyed and you quarrel. I do understand, but I'm new here, and you must give me a little time, for I do want to help you. I realize only too well how you feel.'

The woman stared at her for a moment, mechanically wiping her hands on a creased old apron on which she had done this before. Then she stammered out what she was thinking. 'I didn't want no lady doctor. It isn't the right job for a lady, it isn't, but you does understand a lot better than them other doctors. I will say that.'

'I want to help you,' Anna said, and she hoped that this comforted her, for she needed it.

By the end of the week she had found a small home in a back street of the town itself. It was clean, and conformed to pattern, and Miss Willis said that they were kind people. The farm cart came in every market day, and then they could visit him. She went over to the farm again, and now she knew that the woman trusted her implicitly, and she met the man, for whom she did not care quite so much, but he was not opposing in any way. He was only too glad to get rid of the father-in-law, and thought that she must be a splendid doctor to have. They made the arrangements.

Four days later they got the old man into the home, and that very evening Anna received a telephone call from the clergyman in whose parish the family lived. His name was Hugh Felton, she was told, and he sounded about thirty years old; he apologized for being husky, but he had only one lung working properly, and had had to live in the country for the fresh air that he got there. The woman at the farm had told him of Anna. 'I'm sorry about the recommend,' he laughed, 'but this is the way we do things in the country.'

He had been sawing up some logs for his ever-demanding open fire, and the saw had slipped and had cut him fairly badly; could she get to him?

She gathered that he thought she was working with Drs Webb and Higgs, and she put him straight on that. He seemed quite pleased.

'That's all the better,' he said. 'Do please come along.'

She went out straight away to a countrified rectory, the sagging gate propped wide open (it had long ago given up shutting properly), and the large but comfortable house standing right back. It was a nasty wound, but she stitched it up. 'And don't touch the dressing till I return to do it the day after tomorrow,' she warned him.

He was not far from her own age, with amused eyes, and a merry personality. He took life as being something of a joke; if you didn't, it would kill you, he explained. He was annoyed that he must not garden for some time, for half the men from the village had gone, and he could get so little help. There was quite a lot to do, for the rectory was far too big for him, and the garden huge. Then he asked, 'What do I owe you? I'd rather pay as I go along.'

'Please don't worry about that. Let me get it right first. I'll come round the day after tomorrow. Give it a chance to heal, but if it goes on hurting too much, ring me,' and she pushed a card of hers on to the side table where the telephone stood.

He was a nice man (she liked him), but she realized that this sort of practice could hardly pay for the weekly joint. It was going to be difficult to get herself properly established, of course, for some people would resent the fact that she had been forced to put up her plate. It was *not* the way to start, but there was no going back on that, for she had bought the house, and there was nothing else that she could have done. She had a few hundreds behind her, no more, and whatever happened she had to get the practice going quickly, before the other two doctors returned home, and they were the favourites, she learnt, coming back as national heroes.

She had already discovered that everybody in the town seemed to dislike the medical men in it. They told her that the only worthwhile doctors had joined up in the 'war to end all wars'. Now she had to earn money to live, for the house had taken all her savings.

Her brand-new plate flashed like gold, for Miss Willis took a pride in it, and she had a morning surgery which was little more than a waste of time, for few came to it. She did confide her anxiety to Hugh Felton, the parson at the big country rectory. He told her that she must give luck a chance, that was only fair.

She very much liked the little market town tucked into the valley, with a rather reluctant river whispering its way through it, but medically it was hopelessly old-fashioned. How any of the inhabitants had managed to live so long made her wonder.

It was now obvious that the war would end in a few weeks, almost days. Certainly it would be over by Christmas, and as soon as it could be arranged the two trusted doctors would return. Then it might not be so easy for her. She knew this only too well.

'I do wish I knew what to do,' she told herself.

But early in November she found a trump card in her hand.

Lord Porth lived in a large handsome house a good three miles outside the town. It stood in a magnificent deer park, and he sent for her. Anna knew from a talk with Miss Willis (who was very good at always knowing what lay behind the scenes, and what was going on, with a bit more added for luck!), and she said that he had been divorced by his first wife, and had married the present Lady Porth in something of a hurry, for their first child, a son, and heir to the title, was born just after! He was the veritable apple of their eyes.

Apparently he had come on with what his nanny and his mother called politely 'tummy-ache', and they sent for Anna.

She knew, of course (Miss Willis again), that they had quarrelled with the old doctors Webb and Higgs, and had been some time waiting in hope for what they called 'new blood'.

She went at once.

A footman let her in, and Lord Porth, an extremely nice man, greeted her. The child was in far too much pain, they thought, and did not know what to do. She went up to him and found an advanced appendix! She knew that time was running out, for they said he had been 'grizzling for two or three days', and she rather thought it had been going on longer than they said. It should be operated on this morning.

Now she met with opposition!

Whoever operated must be the best man in London (money was no object at all), and they wanted Sir Thomas James, who also happened to be a friend of theirs. They got in touch on the telephone. Anna was now extremely worried for her patient, for the surgeon could not possibly get here until the late afternoon, when anything *could* have happened.

She said to his father, 'You must understand that this is a case of the sooner the better, and it *is* a very simple operation to do. He has had this pain now for four days at least, and is getting worse. I want to operate immediately.'

They wished Sir Thomas to do it, and said so. She was not happy about this, but they had phoned, and Sir Thomas would be on the late-afternoon train. She nodded. 'I should like to stay with the boy,' she said. 'He must be carefully watched.'

'His nanny . . .' began Lord Porth.

She said, 'His nanny is not trained in the way of appendices go; I *am*. I want to be sure the child lives!'

She knew that the way she said it alarmed him, but she had meant it to do this. The boy ought to be operated on right now, and she said so. At two in the afternoon he was worse, and she went down to the parents. Now she was mistress of the situation, and all doctor.

She said, 'Now look here! If the little lad is to live, that operation has to be done right now! It has already gone too far, and I dare not wait, for if we are too late the boy will die, whoever does it. I have got to get it out before it bursts—*now*.'

There must have been something about the way that she said it, the determination, for she made them agree. When it came to fighting for a life, in particular a child's life, she was most determined. They had a doctor friend who would give the anaesthetic, and she asked for a well-scrubbed kitchen table. It might seem to be ignoble for the heir to so much, but she had done this before. They rigged up the big bathroom as a theatre and she rushed the operation. She had to be careful, for she was only just in time; she had never seen a nastier appendix, and in another hour anything could have happened.

But she *did* it, it was a sheer miracle that she had persuaded the parents in time, the boy would have died if they had held out. When the great Sir Thomas arrived she would have the appendix ready to show him! She had never operated in quite such challenging circumstances before, nor on a so much wanted heir, and she understood how they all felt.

Sir Thomas James was brought to the park later, in a large car which had been sent to meet him. The child had not yet come round. Anna knew of him as being a magnificent lecturer, and she had admired his work, and the help that he gave to students, but he was a man who stood for no nonsense when it came to question-time.

He saw the unconscious child, and came down to the drawing-room again with Anna, where Lord and Lady Porth were waiting for them.

He said, 'Your son owes his life to Dr Thorpe. If she had held back, I should have been too late, for it was almost bursting when she got the thing out,' and he beamed.

Anna felt her own heart quickening. It had been a tricky operation, for she knew how dangerous it was, and she had used the most extreme care. She told Sir Thomas the difficulty she had had in persuading the parents, but she had done it in the end. Privately she wondered what on earth the great man would charge, for he had the reputation of asking the most tremendous fees, and she smiled as she thought of it.

He asked her about her practice in Weston. 'You are a partner with some old-established firm, I presume?'

She wished that she did not blush so easily. She told him the truth. The first idea had been to join forces with an old-established firm (she did not admit how moth-eaten they were), and she had come down to see them and believed that all was well, so had bought herself a charming house here. In the end they had not wanted her, and said so most coldly. A nephew of one of them had managed to qualify most unexpectedly, for he had already failed on four previous occasions, she believed, and they had taken him instead.

'You mean they turned down an FRCS?' Sir Thomas asked her.

She laughed at that. 'I think they wanted to keep the practice in the family, and maybe there they were wise! So I could only put up my plate.'

It was Lord Porth who spoke to her. 'After

this you are going to be our doctor, and don't you forget it! We will send for you every time. We have been searching for a decent doctor ever since we got here, but the war took the two good ones away, and it was by sheer luck that we heard about you. Matron at the hospital told us of you. She knew you would help.'

'We felt that Eddie was safe with you looking after him,' Lady Porth said, and somehow the girl knew that this was one of the greatest compliments she had ever had.

The great man had to catch the next train back, and before she went home Anna visited her patient again. He was coming round, was rather weepy, and said that he wanted a chocolate cream.

'That,' Anna told his mother, 'is a very good sign. Oh no, he didn't get it, of course, but it tells me that he is going to be all right.'

Lord Porth insisted on her accepting a big cheque before she finally left. She had thought of charging £25 (a fortune to her, and she did not want to overdo it). He said that was rubbish, and he pressed a cheque for £100 into her hand, so that she drove home in a complete daze. Never had she had such a pleasant shock in her life! As she opened the door of her house, Miss Willis came to greet her with enthusiasm.

'They do say that the war is almost over, Doctor,' she said. 'It really is ending now.'

Anna slumped down into a hall chair looking at Miss Willis as if she had not seen her. She said, 'Everything is happening today. Every mortal thing,' and she felt quite helpless with it. 'I wonder if it is true.'

'The paper says so.'

It seemed unbelievable! Although it had lasted for only four years, it seemed to her to have been an eternity of time. What a relief to learn that it was nearly over! But the end would mean that the two reliable doctors whom the town loved and trusted would then be coming back. It might mean an end to the progress she had made so far.

When she visited the Porth heir next day he was remarkably well. She was happy about him, and excited to hear the noise in Weston as the whole town went mad with the announcement of the armistice. Now there were no fears of an air raid, or the sound of bombs which had always given her the jitters in London, though she had kept up a brave front. And there could never be another war like it, for this had been fought with courage and with bitter losses.

Now a new world opened its doors to her.

As she went on her rounds, Anna felt that

this would be a turn in the whole life of the town. So far, she had done much better than she had ever thought to be possible, because she had had luck, and comparatively no competition. There had been four patients in her surgery this morning and, considering the very short time it was since she had been forced to put up her plate, she thought that this was rather good.

She listened to the noise of a world gone crazy now that peace had come. Thank God war could never come again, she thought. We had lost too many, and worked too hard.

The small town was in a state of rare excitement. From somewhere or other flags had been brought out, and the somewhat dejected buildings, which had never had a single hour of repair work since the August of 1914, had these little flags on them, and some paper chains and such.

When she returned to lunch, Miss Willis was in a great state of perturbation. Apparently Dr Webb had been taken ill, they had sent in for help, but Anna was on her rounds, and in the end another rather aged doctor, who was supposed to have retired, had been called in. The old gentleman had been found unconscious on his bedroom floor, and he had died two hours later.

'Another stroke, I suppose,' said Miss Willis.

* * *

The story of the Porths' son's appendix had gone the rounds, and everybody knew that Anna had operated whilst the great surgeon was on his way, and had saved the boy's life. This thrilled the town. It was just the sort of story that they loved, and it helped her. She had never realized how busily small towns talked, and of course the fact that she was a woman doctor was in itself very interesting. But she was still self-reproachful at having had to put up her plate, though it had been forced on her. Now she found her practice growing bigger and bigger.

Maybe people came to her because she was new, or they wanted to see what she was like, but the rumour had got around that at last somebody had arrived who could save life. This changed the pattern.

She was alarmed at the thought of established men returning, for they would be back in practice before three months at the most were up, and this was a problem.

But since the Porth heir had been saved (and almost at the last minute), her surgery filled. People were there every day waiting for her, and she got more and more calls.

There came a request from Lady Esmay, who lived on the far side of the town in a magnificent country-house, standing in parkland. Anna knew of her, for Miss Willis had kept her informed! She was a mine of information. Lord Esmay had gone off with another woman, leaving his wife and her only child, a seven-year-old daughter named Alison, who was down with flu.

Anna herself took the call. 'I'll come,' she said.

When she got there, Lady Esmay greeted her. She had wanted to change her doctor ever since the war began, but so far there had been nobody to whom she *could* change. She thought the child had flu, that ambiguous title which the ordinary layman puts to any odd illness going the rounds. When Anna got into the night nursery she knew instantly that this was the dreaded flu from which far more people had died than had been killed during the whole of the war.

She ordered two nurses to be with the child, and visited her twice a day. She found that Lady Esmay was the most charming woman, in the early thirties, and very worried. She was nervous and shy, and apparently had few friends to whom she could turn.

The raging flu which had suddenly surged through Europe, with the most staggering death-toll, had taken far too many lives. It was rampant in the town, and Anna had a heavy visiting list. Many of the patients she could not save, the infection was too acute, and the trouble was that everybody was weakened by four years of insufficient food.

Now her surgery was full. Everyone wanted her.

By Christmas the Esmay child had rounded the corner, and Anna took a few hours off duty. Lord Porth had sent her the sort of turkey that would occupy the larder for three weeks! She felt much happier about life, and went over to hear Hugh Felton preach his Christmas sermon, which she thought would do her good.

It had been a momentous autumn for her, a time when everything seemed to have happened, and she had dared to set up her plate, and was now actually surviving. But she was worried that the two popular doctors would soon be back. They were the trusted friends of everybody.

The late Dr Webb's nephew had come next door, a man with a limp handshake that inspired none. A doctor should give confidence, and he was not the man to do this. Too fond of the pubs, said Miss Willis.

On New Year's Eve Anna saw the new year in, as she had always done at home. Undoubtedly she would be called out the moment she had gone to bed, and then regret having sat up. She heard the church bells ringing in the first year of real peace, and of course there could never be another war! The dying year had been the most eventful of her entire life. She had done the right thing in coming here, and she loved the house, but she saw ahead of her a host of difficult times, and was afraid for 1919. She had to remember that there were still numbers of people, especially in the provincial world, who disliked the idea of a woman doctor. But this *was* a new year, and she had it in her own power to make it a good one.

The little Esmay girl had been very seriously ill for four days, and Anna herself had had qualms that she might not recover. It was a winter with a lot of illness, undoubtedly caused by malnutrition, for nobody had had the right sort of food to eat. Little Alison was the only child of the first of her father's three marriages; Miss Willis knew that he was a flirtatious man, and a difficult one, who in the end had gone off with a very common girl from the neighbourhood, and had eventually married her. The marriage had produced one of those problems which interested the entire town for weeks. Things had had to be speeded up because the girl was pregnant, and when her son was born he was black! She had, so report said, been having a previous affair with a young American, a coloured man, who had been with those singers who originally introduced ragtime to England.

What Lord Esmay was doing about it, and whether her Ladyship would remain her Ladyship or not, had set the entire town talking.

Anna felt deeply sorry for his first wife, the gentle, very quiet mother of Alison. She rejoiced on the day when she came down the stairs to tell the mother that Alison would be all right now.

'She will live,' she said as she entered the octagonal drawing-room where Lady Esmay sat forlornly by the fire. 'She may be delicate for a time, and when you can you ought to take her to a warmer climate for the spring. The south of France, perhaps, somewhere with sun,' and then she added: 'It would do you good, also, for you have had all the worry and the wretchedness.'

'You've been most awfully helpful.'

'That is what I am here for,' and Anna smiled. 'Don't fret, and do take a tonic from me, to help you get over the worrying. When a child gets as ill as Alison has been, the mother also gets ill as a rule.'

She wrote out a prescription.

She drove home through the bright clear light of a new year, and she realized that on the whole she had been extremely lucky. In 1918 it was not easy for a woman doctor to get herself established; many people felt that she usurped a man's job; she would be all right in a children's hospital or something like that, but not as a doctor in a general practice. But fate had forced her to come, and she was making good. She was coming to be accepted, and some influential people in the neighbourhood had turned to her and were delighted with her services.

The new doctor next door was not popular, lazy, never came when called, and, as Miss Willis put it, 'drank like a fish', and she vowed that she had once seen him being pushed home drunk in a wheelbarrow, very late at night, and she swore that this was true.

'I am not quite through the wood yet,' Anna told herself, though with Lord Porth and Lady Esmay she knew that she had laid a couple of fairly substantial foundation stones for the future of her practice.

If determination could make good, she *would* get there. She felt that there could probably be a living for all of them, and she hoped for the best. She had dug herself in a little, but it was still going to be hard work. She had got to realize this.

Early in the January of the new year she was called out to Dr Brown. Report had it that he had never been seen completely sober for years. He had suffered a bad fall in a back-street public house, the sort of place in which she would not have thought he would have wished to be seen, but where apparently he constantly went.

He had gone in for a drink, had had trouble with a man he did not like, and had tripped. He had broken an arm, and she thought that he had badly injured a leg, but could not imagine why they had sent for her. She was a newcomer, and would have thought that the others would have been better able to help him. She got him into hospital, and there suggested that they sent for his own doctor, who was Dr Higgs.

'I was just the doctor they got in an emergency,' she explained to Matron.

The patient must have heard what she said, for he opened his eyes, and grinning to her said, 'You'll do me proud. I have always liked pretty girls!'

This was not really very helpful.

When she left him, she reported to Dr Higgs (who, Matron told her, 'usually helped him out'), but from the letter that Dr Higgs sent her she gathered that he was none too pleased over what had happened. Next evening she enquired after him, and learned that he was not at all well; he died two days later.

She worried about this, though she did not think that anything could have been done to save him. The habitual drunk goes steadily on until something catches up with him, and then there is very little that one can do. Miss Willis told her that worry never got anyone very far, and it was better to forget these things. She had always felt that Anna took her career too much to heart.

With the new spring, and at peace, the first of the two doctors had returned, a married man, and she had met his nice wife and four children. She found him amiable; he liked knowing new people, and thought there was plenty of room for all of them, so was glad that she had come here. He was friendly, and, although he did not actually put this into words, she inferred that he thought new blood was necessary, and the town needed someone fresh in it. He would avail himself of her surgery, he said. She knew from what she had heard about him in the town that he would be a help.

'I've been fortunate,' she told herself, 'and now I have a real hope of quietly building up a practice here. It may mean the waiting game, but I have sufficient courage to face it, and so far I have had a lot of luck.'

CHAPTER TWO

Old Sir George Bell changed his doctor and came to her. She had been warned that he could be quite the most troublesome patient that she was ever likely to meet, and so used to getting his own way about everything that she would regret it.

'Given time, I'll be all right,' she told herself, for time is a great help in almost everything. She knew that the small town had been glad to get a new doctor. The old custom of a doctor living to a ripe old age, and then dying in his practice, seemed to have been the routine here.

Already Anna had a regular surgery which was growing all the time. She had a small but faithful list of patients, which was increasing, for she was gentle, and the woman found it easier to talk to another woman than to a man, especially of the kind as typified by Doctors Webb and Higgs.

Anna realized that she was living down the vague apprehension which had filled some people about women in medicine.

Then suddenly she had got a call from Hugh Felton. When she turned in at his gate and rang the doorbell, she was surprised to see him limping.

'It is awfully good of you to come,' he said. 'I should not have bothered you, but to tell you the truth I gave my leg a bad knock, and that seems to have started it off again, and I've got to the point where I can't stick it any longer. I have no regular doctor, for I have not been here long enough.'

They went into the large, rather messy dining-room, and she saw that he was limping very badly. She immediately guessed what the trouble was and remembered that recently a new form of treatment had been discovered which was said to be doing great things. It would mean an operation, and she knew that men were more difficult to persuade than women, but it was the only way out. He should have sent for her before.

Hugh Felton was amiable. He made her some coffee because it was a cold day, and he felt that she needed something to 'warm the cockles'.

Before the house spread a large garden, which had gone fairly wild, but the elm trees were thickening with pale pink blossom, one of the first flowers of the new year. She loved the view across the valley beyond it, and then the hills rising. When summer came it must be a glorious place in which to live.

'How welcome the coffee is!' she said. 'Our stove at home went wrong last night, and we haven't been able to get anything hot this morning. I left Miss Willis trying to cope.'

'I've met her, and I'd think she *could* cope. I notice that stoves always go wrong when the weather is really cold. It is one of their habits.'

'Yes, I know.'

She mentioned the big bowl of laurustinus which was standing in the centre of the table, the white forerunner of other flowers to come, and she remembered that it had been her mother's favourite flower, though she could not think why. She herself thought it rather dull, even if it did come first of all the shrubs. He adored flowers and admitted that the large garden was why he had accepted the living. He loved working in it, but now that his leg was being so difficult, he could do very little. She explained that he ought to have an operation, or he would be left permanently lame, and the sooner he had it the better. But every woman doctor knows how hard it is to persuade a man to do anything, even for his own good, when it may cause suffering.

'It is curable only if you do what I say, and we shall have to act quickly,' she told him.

There was no other cure. He ought to have

sent for her as soon as he knocked it.

'You want to operate?' he asked her.

'I'm being honest when I tell you that if you leave it you will become very lame, and you can't afford to take that risk.'

He paused, then surprisingly he said, 'Right! Let's get it over straight away. When can you do it? And what will it cost?'

She appreciated the calm matter-of-fact manner in which he accepted what must have been a nasty shock to him, and she hesitated before she spoke again.

'If you have the operation done in hospital, you would not have to pay a heavy fee, and Matron is a nice woman. I think you would be there about three weeks, that is if everything goes well, as it should do.'

He was entirely practical about it, and she liked his courage, for she had to confess that there would be a good deal of pain, though she would control it as much as she could.

They talked of other things too. He had been to Cambridge at the very college where her own father had been before he turned to medicine, and this seemed to be something of a link between them. He had no objection to being treated by a woman doctor, and said that he thought it had been very brave of her to put up her plate when the old doctors had let her down so badly.

She smiled at that.

'Really I did not have an awful lot of choice,' she said. 'I'd bought the house, and the furniture in it, and too late found out that they did not want me.'

'Well, you have courage, and there seems to be room for a good doctor in the town, from all I can hear. I admire your determination, and if you can put this darned leg right for me, I shall admire it even more!'

They made the arrangements in an entirely prosaic manner; she could arrange it, and let him have news the day after tomorrow. Would that do? She felt his calmness most commendable, for not all men accept a painful operation quite so easily.

As she drove home she had the feeling that he would be a very good patient, and prayed that she would make a real success of it. It was not an operation that she would like doing, it could so easily produce complications, but she was prepared for them. As she drove the car home she prayed that it would be *the* big success of her life.

The matron was a kind woman, and most helpful. Anna made all the arrangements that afternoon, and on Matron's suggestion obtained the services of a very good anaesthetist, from a small town on the other side of Weston. She was returning from the hospital to ring Hugh Felton up about it, when she saw Dr Higgs walking towards her, with that rather sickly smile of his as though he had something to say. She had spoken to him only once since the day when she had first come to the town to enquire about joining his practice, and she could not think what he wanted now.

'Good afternoon,' she said, and she hoped that it sounded amiable.

'And how are we getting on?' he asked in the solicitous manner of an aged uncle to a niece who he privately thinks is rather spoilt.

'Oh, I'm bearing up,' she told him. 'I realize that I did the wrong thing, but I had no choice, had I?'

He still smirked at her, and murmured something that she did not quite catch. She changed the subject.

'I was sorry that Dr Webb died so suddenly,' she told him.

He shrugged his shoulders. 'Possibly that is the easiest way,' he said, and quickly he in turn changed the subject. 'I have always felt that we missed something in not getting you as third in the practice,' and again he smirked. 'Webb's nephew is with me now,' and by the tone of his voice she gathered that the partnership was not entirely satisfactory. As she said nothing, he changed his tone. 'Somewhat naturally, I never expected you to put up your plate.'

The one thing she did not want was to have a row, for that would be absurd, something of a disaster. She said rather sadly, 'I'm sorry about that, but I had bought the house, which you suggested I should do, if you remember, and needs must when the devil drives,' then she walked past him, and into her own house. Whatever happened she must break the conversation, or there *would* be a row.

At this time she had to admit that her patients were on the increase, and she was doing quite well. She felt relieved that she was rounding the difficult corners, and it was just about now that Dr Adams suddenly appeared. She saw him walking across the road to her, just as she was getting into her car for some country visits. He held out a hand.

'Hello, Doctor!' he said. 'How pleasant to meet you again. I hear you are doing well here, and it *is* a change to have a woman working here with us.' He had the most pleasant smile.

'That's very kind of you,' she said, 'for I did

put up my plate.'

'I know, and if you ask me, it makes me laugh! You were wanted here. My goodness, the war let this town down, I wonder all the inhabitants didn't die! You did very well with the Porth heir.'

She said, 'Thank you,' very quietly.

'And now old Webb's nephew has joined up with Dr Higgs, and I should think that will be the end. You've met him?' and when she said no, he laughed and said, 'You *are* in for fun!'

He was a charming man who said what he thought, and instinctively she was amused by him. She felt that they would not be rivals, but real friends, and so far she had had the underlying feeling that the doctors resented her, because she *was* a woman, and this was a time when women doctors were not too popular in the profession.

But she did have the very strong support of Matron at the hospital, and of Hugh Felton, on whose leg she was to operate. He really was the most helpful patient to have, entirely trusting her. A man who hid his feelings very well, but although he seemed to be so keen on the operation originally, she did think that his enthusiasm was slightly cooling down now, and she sympathized with him. She ought, perhaps, to have told him nothing about the pain of the first four days, but she had thought it only fair to give him due warning. Then the condition of the leg got worse; he had a bad attack of pain, so much so that a friend had to take his place on the Sunday, and in the end the operation had to be rushed.

Two days later Anna operated.

She knew that it was ridiculous to be nervous about it, but she just couldn't help it. It is so much easier to operate on strangers than on a friend. As she entered the theatre, she told herself that this makes all the difference in the world. In hospital one merely operates on bodies; in private practice one is always operating on people whom one knows, and undoubtedly this does make it more heart-rending to the surgeon.

It was a very much more difficult operation than she had anticipated, for unexpected complications had set in. She felt so very sorry for him; he was too nice a man to have to go through this.

In the end the operation took a great deal longer than it should have done, and she was worried over it. But she did it well, leaving nothing to chance, for she had found that in surgery chance is always against one.

It finished with the ever-familiar sound of the trolley taking the unconscious patient back to bed.'

It was the anaesthetist who spoke to her with a grin spread all over his cheerful face. 'That was pretty hot!' he said, 'it had gone further than you had expected, hadn't it?'

'You're right there, it *had*! But I happened to deal with this particular operation in my finals, and have done it many times since, so that was a help.'

He nodded. 'I'd never have tried it myself, but you got him round that corner, I must say. I'm the dead ordinary GP, sometimes go the rounds on a bike, which is a bit old-fashioned, and I am never the big-job chap,' and he laughed at the idea.

She said quietly, 'The saving of life is always a big job, and you have done that. Don't underrate your capacity.'

He preened himself.

Matron had arranged for them to have tea in her little sitting-room. When Matron talked her tongue ran away with her. They discussed the nephew who had joined Dr Higgs in his practice, and had filled the gap caused by Dr Webb's death. He had had luck in stepping right into that, but he seemed to be a dilatory young man, always late on his visits, and not interested in small-town life, which surely was an essential here.

Anna had had luck, especially with the Porth boy, but now with the war well over, and the other two doctors returning, one of them already back, it would probably be a very different story. She was feeling tired, more so, she thought, than she had ever felt before, and she played with a dream. If she could get away for Easter it would be quite a good thing to do. She had already given too much to the practice.

By Mothering Sunday both of the doctors were back in their own homes again, and they were far nicer and friendlier men than she had expected. She had been privately alarmed lest they disliked the idea of a woman doctor stepping into the gap, and actually putting up her plate. She had not realized that nobody at all had liked the Webb and Higgs partnership, and everyone was rather glad to have new blood.

Perhaps Anna was one of those people who are inclined to exaggerate their apprehensions, which is no wise way in which to go through life, only her position here had been, as she put it herself, 'just a wee bit sticky'. Now it was definitely improving.

Dr Richard Graves, who returned with the MC, was a particularly amiable man, she had thought unmarried, but the Matron—who

:w everything—told her that his wife had run off with another man ('So disgraceful, just a grocer!') before the war, and Dr Graves had divorced her.

'I never liked her,' said Matron, 'nor did I like the chap she went off with; he "did" me once, and that is the sort of thing I never forget.'

*   *   *

Anna had become aware of the fact that the demands of the winter and founding her practice had been a strain. Now morning and evening surgeries brought their little bands of patients; where originally she had put some of it down to sheer curiosity, now she knew that it was more than this. They liked her and appreciated her skill.

It was Miss Willis who suggested that she should take the Easter weekend off, for it had been a six months' grind, and Miss Willis was quite right. Anna had the inspiration of going down to the Isle of Wight, for there the spring comes early.

'That's a very good idea, Doctor,' said Miss Willis. 'I can manage here for you, and you can't go on working day and night as you've been doing ever since you first started up practice here.'

Anna knew that she had already established herself, and well. The two doctors back from the front were in practice again, both of them proving to be very sensible men, and friendly too. They would help her out. Whatever she felt about it privately, ever since Christmas she *had* worked very hard. The Porth boy's appendix had started the ball rolling. She had kept the appendix in a bottle in the surgery, as a mascot for her, though not for the world would she have admitted this to anyone, and she only hoped that Miss Willis did not know. Then there had been the little Esmay child, who had so nearly died. She and her mother were in Bournemouth, and Anna received delightful picture postcards from them. And now she needed a breathing space. 'I simply *must* have a few days off,' she told herself.

CHAPTER THREE

Anna went away, with Dr Richard Graves standing in for her. She went to Ventnor, which she had visited when she was a child, and she loved it, for the Isle of Wight is so entirely different from the mainland. Her mother had adored it. On Tennyson Downs she had said she always had the impression that she walked on the most extravagant velvet carpet.

Anna *meant* to make this entirely different, because she had arrived at the stage when she dreamed of the night bell whenever she got to bed, and the practice was beginning to get slightly on her nerves. She knew that she worried too much, but she had been born this way, and it is not easy to curb this habit. For a long weekend she would forget everything, she told herself.

She needed this change.

Travelling in that ridiculous little train across the island to Ventnor, she realized that it had not altered and was much the same as she remembered it. This was all to the good, for there are so few places to which you can go back and find them as you remember them.

The hotel was not grand, but very comfortable, and had a pleasant garden round it, with flowers out well in advance of those in the Midlands. Next morning she walked out and on to Tennyson Downs, which she had always recalled with affection. They were unchanged, and that was a joy. This was the first time that she found herself able to forget the practice, and relax. A very blue sea lay beneath her, and the soft grass was under her feet.

It was then that she met Robin Grant.

They were, as far as she could see, the only two people walking on the downs on this very lovely early spring morning. He raised his cap, said 'Good morning,' and smiled as though they were old friends.

One of the curious things in life is that there are strangers whom you meet almost *as* old friends, like people you have not seen since schooldays, and this was what happened now. Of course, she had never seen him before, yet impulsively she welcomed him as being a friend.

Yet there was a certain familiarity about his face, she had the idea that she *had* seen him somewhere before, then dismissed the idea as being quite ridiculous. When he gave her his name, Robin Grant, she instantly knew that he was playing the lead at the Shaftesbury Theatre, and could not think how he had managed to get away for this Easter weekend. He said that he had been ill, nothing much, a bad cold which threatened his voice, and that would be a disaster for him, so, acting on medical advice, he had come down here for a long weekend to try to remedy things.

When he said it she recalled that she had read somewhere something about 'a small breakdown' in the papers, but he looked well enough. He was a tall man with very fair hair, such as a girl would have envied, and which contrasted strangely with dark brown eyes, and the sort of complexion that those same girls would also have envied.

He said, 'Isn't this a glorious morning? and whenever I come down here it seems to be this way. Not a soul about; there is a lovely isolation about Tennyson Downs.'

She agreed. She told him that she had not been here since she was a child, and somehow it was just as she had remembered it. They walked on the grass which is like thick velvet, under their feet, and the huge memorial just ahead of them.

'You work?' he asked her.

She laughed at that. 'Do I not! It's a

ghastly confession to have to make, but I'm a doctor!'

'Surely not?' He said it with great surprise, and repeated quickly, 'Surely not?'

'I most certainly am.'

'Good heavens! Now I'm an actor.'

'Yes, I know, I saw you once. Now that is the sort of job I could never do.'

'And medicine would play hell with me! I'm one of those chaps who turn funny at the sight of blood.'

'One gets over that,' she told him. 'If I were on the stage, frankly I should be terrified. That awful curtain going slowly up, and myself facing the enormous theatre. That *would* stun me.'

'But why? You are not yourself, you are somebody else for the time being, and this is exciting. You may be a bully, or a sneak, a coward, or a lover. I always wanted to act, and believe me, it was *not* easy to persuade my mother, who wanted the Navy for me, because she thought it such a gentlemanly profession! You know what mothers are!'

He interested her.

She admitted she would never have got her own mother to let her go in for medicine if her father had not been a doctor before her, so she believed it was something of an 'inheritance'.

They walked some way together, talking with that casual calm which sometimes comes to total strangers, and which can be quite enthralling. They shared opinions and attitudes to life. They spoke of the sheer horror of the war just past, and then all the men coming back with gratuities and no jobs, but the one thing was certain—this was the end of war in Europe for ever. It could *never* happen again.

'I wonder,' he said. 'As long as a small baby hits another small baby with his rattle, there must always be wars. Man lives this way, he always has done, and always will.'

'I only hope you are wrong,' she said.

He was a most interesting man, and they talked as if they were old friends, not strangers who had met quite casually walking over the downs. Then he asked her to dine and dance with him at his hotel that night. She knew that it was a big hotel, quite a way from Ventnor, but he would fetch her in his car.

On the spur of the moment she said, 'I'd love it.'

When she got back to her own hotel and thought more of it, she felt that the whole meeting had been rather odd. It was quite unusual for her to talk to a complete stranger like this, and to arrange to go dancing with him. Today her profession had not walked with her, as it generally did; she was devoted to her work, and always tried to conform to the demands that it made on her; but this morning she had been a very ordinary young girl, meeting a very ordinary young man, and talking to him in an ordinary way. Then she told herself, 'I'm on holiday, why shouldn't I enjoy myself?' He had, in the vulgar language of *hoi polloi*, picked her up. He had spoken to her on Tennyson Downs, the only people in sight, and it had seemed to be quite natural. 'I *shall* go tonight,' she told herself, 'anything for a change.'

She had had a ghastly winter, when she came to think of it, for she had been so terribly worried lest she did not make good. There had been such a lot at stake. She had bought the charming house, believing she would be third in a fairly solid partnership, only to find that she was nothing of the sort, and after all they did not want her. She had always felt that a woman doctor was very much on her own, because most of the men doctors seemed to be suspicious of them, but with the war on, she perhaps had had a better chance.

The war was over now. What next?

She wondered what to wear tonight, and it was such a time since she had done this. She had two evening dresses with her, one of which was more 'late afternoon', but the other a dream dress that she had bought in a fit of madness when she got her Fellowship. It was a soft blue dress, with a wide fichu to it, and a single pale pink rose tucked into the chiffon. Suddenly, in an entirely new mood, she chose it, because it removed her further from the woman doctor line, and made her look rather pretty. She was ashamed to admit this, but it was true.

She was the girl standing on the threshold of life, maybe she had worked so hard, and had worried so much about it all, that she did not recognize the figure in the wardrobe glass which was really herself.

'It can't be true! I look so different,' she thought.

'Maybe a dream comes into one's life only once in a while, and when it does come it is wise to make the most of it and to enjoy it,' she told herself. He called for her fairly early, and they went out to the very handsome car together. They drove through that glorious unspoilt country of the island, and entered a wide avenue which led to the hotel. To her it was the height of luxury, something which she had never really tasted, for hers had been a hard life, making do all the time. After all, as she told herself, scraping through big exams, and living on hospital food, is not too much luxury! She told him about it.

'I was just working for my finals on a few pence a week,' she said.

'Did you get through? I've always heard it can be a bit elusive.'

'Indeed it can, but I had luck. I got a lot of questions about the gall-bladder operation. I had had a spot of bother with one of them only the week before, and that helped me. I never put a foot wrong. Just luck. It isn't often that exams are so kind to one.'

'Looking at you, I should never have guessed you were a doctor.'

She took that as being a great compliment, and she smiled. 'Sailors show their job because they roll, soldiers show it because somehow they never get away from marching, but doctors are not so easily spotted, thank heaven. Some women doctors try to look like men, but I always think that is a mistake. I prefer to be just myself.'

He had ordered champagne, and they sat there talking. She enquired about his career. His father had been an actor, trained with Sir Frank Benson's company, but on the whole he did rather badly. He went in for Shakespeare and all the heavy stuff, no wonder he had died young! His mother had prayed that her only child would not want to go on the stage, for she had had enough of back-street digs and tiresome landladies who demanded the rent before pay night, and of severe retrenchment. The one thing that she had hoped was that her one son would do something 'respectable'. But he himself had wanted the stage when in the mid-teens, and had become quite successful.

He said, 'I always think that if you very much want a job, then you go through with it. I never looked back. Got an understudy part, and the very first night the chap slipped on a step and broke an ankle. His luck was out, but mine was in!'

She too had had luck, she said, but not so much luck when she tried to get into a practice, and now with the war over, and all the good men coming back into competition, the luck might not be quite as bright.

'So far it *is* all right,' she admitted.

'And now the old faithfuls have returned?'

'That is exactly it!'

He hesitated, and then he said, 'Remember that tomorrow is always another day,' and quietly left it at that. She knew that she interested him, and in turn she asked about his work. He had gone to a fairly cheap school, though from there he got a scholarship for a better one. He owed all his luck to one of the masters there, the brother of a famous actor, who recognized the gift in this boy one Christmas, when they were doing the end-of-term play. He had encouraged him.

It was the encouragement of that amiable young school-master that sent him to a drama school and enabled him to put his first foot on the ladder. It had been a hard grind, of course, and he never got very far until the actor he was understudying broke his ankle. In a flash Robin was on the next step.

As the curtain went up, he told himself, 'I've got to do better than he did,' and that was exactly what happened. When one is very young, enthusiasm drives hard.

'This is a game of chance,' he said. 'Opportunity knocks on the door, and it may perhaps be disguised as some old tramp; it always comes in the unexpected manner, but it *does* come.'

She thought of Eddie Porth's appendix, and the specialist racing down, and herself taking action. That had been *her* opportunity, she told herself.

He laughed as he went on talking of his career, how his mother said that she had always known that he would do well, which d never known, and how the headmaster said that he had seen it coming, which again was untrue. He had made good at an extremely early age.

'You must come and see the show on your way back. You could break the journey in London,' he said.

She should refuse; instead she said, 'That would be quite marvellous.'

'When are you going back?'

'I am going up to London on Tuesday, to do some shopping there, stay the night and go down to the country by the Wednesday afternoon.'

He said, 'I'll tell you what we'll do. I'll take you up with me in my car on Tuesday morning, and then you'll be able to come to the show on Tuesday night. Okay?'

She could hardly believe that any of this was true. Her life had been very much stuck to pattern, working to rule, as all hospital life has to be. She listened to what he said, with the thought that she had entered a new world, somewhere entirely different from anything she had known before. After the show they would dance. (It was the era of dancing, it had come in with the end of the war.) It was something with which she had had little to do so far, for her world had been concentrated on medicine alone. Suddenly she realized that working so hard for her exams, then coming down to the country and putting up her plate, had perhaps asked too much of her. Today was the world of dancing, the tune of 'Alexander's Ragtime Band' ringing in her ears. Then having come into practice with the strangely mixed circumstances which had encompassed her, somehow she seemed to have lost touch with youth. Now the doors opened wide on to a brave new world.

She was grateful that she had brought with her this one good dress, which at the time she had thought to be a silly thing to do, but she had included it because she knew that she felt her best, and looked her best, in it, and she might have the chance to wear it.

All the months in hospital she had been too much set on her work to think of anything else, and she had given every spare moment to study. Now, after a most worrying winter, when she had sat there waiting for the bell to ring, praying that someone really ill would come along, it seemed that her whole world had changed for her.

They danced, and it did not matter if she was late tomorrow, for she would have her breakfast in bed if she so wished it. It seemed that an entirely new personality had come er life and had taken control of her.

Ξ ιhis hour her career had run her life, and had taken complete command of her, day and night, working for, and dreaming of, her forthcoming exams. But now the door had opened for her on to an utterly different world.

She was so late getting back to the hotel that they had closed the door, and someone had to come downstairs to open it up for her.

It was just before one in the morning, and when she looked at herself in the mirror she felt that nothing like this had ever happened to her before. She had for a few hours lived the ordinary life of an ordinary girl, instead of eternally being the doctor on call. Discreet. Guarded, and, in a way, aloof. Tonight she had been herself, and oh, so happy.

She fell asleep with the echo of dance music still throbbing through her, and the joy of being young, and living in a gay new world with that awful war over for ever.

She did not give another thought to the Porth son, or run through the list of patients who would be visiting her this morning had she been at home, for she seemed to have stepped right out of that world, and the practice could look after itself! Nor did she worry herself to death that one of the really good doctors might put an end to her increase in patients.

They would, of course, come back to their old patients, and were, so everybody told her, extremely good, which was more than one could say for those who had stayed behind.

Perhaps she had been very lucky in coming to this place at exactly the right moment last autumn, when the war was gradually fading out and everyone was tired of the doctors who had held the fort and were too old really to hold any fort, and this had been a big help to her. She had come a long way, but still not far enough.

'I shan't worry about that now,' she told herself, for the careless rapture of the moment held her. She was now more woman than doctor at the thought of a change in the town's medical set-up.

Once she had read that there comes a moment in every life when the world changes, and the idea of spending a night in London to break her journey, and of going to the theatre to see Robin Grant act, inspired her. She had thought that the day when she went into the Midlands, and, acting on the spur of the moment, bought the house, settled with Miss Willis, and believed that she would be third partner with the two old doctors, was the of her life. But now she suddenly knew the Easter holiday on the island was in quite another category, and meant far more to her.

It was like some happy dream, one that she enjoyed more than anything else in her life, something that she had snatched from fate after a winter of real hard work, instituting herself in a new job, and settling in.

This was proving to be a very happy weekend, on which she would look back with tender memories. She had needed this rest so much. She would hate returning home again, and she packed her things with reluctance, for this was going to be the end of a dream. She had for a whole long weekend stepped out of a routine which had demanded so much of her. She had been working hard ever since she had started as a medical student, with no real holiday to help her along.

There had never before been the chance to go into her own personal youth and to enjoy it in this way. 'It has been,' she told herself, 'the miracle weekend.'

Robin Grant called for her, and they drove over to the car ferry for the crossing to the mainland. The sea was perfectly calm, for which she was thankful, because she was quite sure that she would be a shockingly bad sailor. When they arrived alongside, they were the first off.

They went out of the town, and up the hill into the beautiful country which lies beyond, through woodlands and peaceful meadows, travelling Londonwards. She was glad to come into the country above the town, and she had the feeling that the most wonderful weekend of her entire life would stay in her memory for ever.

It had been unforgettable.

Gradually they came into London, the hedges slipping away to be replaced by small houses with front gardens, then the shops and the traffic, and no front gardens any more. He dropped her at a hotel he knew, close to the theatre, and told her that they would dine out later.

She found the noise of London a trifle disturbing after the peacefulness of the dear island. She dressed very carefully, knowing that she looked well in her afternoon dress.

She was slightly tired, and had a rest before she joined him. 'Some dreams take a long time to die,' she told herself, for in her own mind this was a dream that could not endure, something entirely different from anything else in her life. In what was merely a handful of hours, he had become an old friend. This was

life worked, she thought. The thing
enjoy the moment, one has only the
present moment to live. It is *now* that matters.

They did not eat before the show, they would go somewhere afterwards, he said, somewhere nice. He could never act if he had a big dinner first, and he had told her about it on the way.

'It takes everyone differently,' was what he said, but she knew that it was something that worried him beforehand, and it must be a heavy strain on the nerves.

He took her in his car to the theatre, dropping her at the front door, with a huge crowd going in, and the buzz and the excitement. She went into the foyer alone. The air was warm, there was the sense of excitement about it, of expectancy and glow, which always comes before a big performance.

Inside the great theatre itself she gave her ticket to the girl who took her to her seat. The stalls were full, it appeared, but more and more seemed to be coming in.

It was a joy to see the house filling, a sensation she had quite forgotten in the years given to her work. She sat there in what seemed to be a new atmosphere, something quite apart from her present life.

It was an excellent play, and undoubtedly

he was a good actor, she would not have known him, and he got a most tremendous reception from the audience. Somehow he seemed to be a different person from the man who had walked on Tennyson Downs with her, the fair hair blowing in the wind, and talking to her as if she were an old friend, and a dear one into the bargain.

He had told her to go behind the scenes to his dressing-room when the show ended, and he sent a programme girl to show her the way. The whole theatre seemed to change in the strange manner that theatres do. The house is all red velvet and gilt and chandeliers, but go through the side door and there you find stone passages, rather grubby walls supposed to be whitewashed, but not living up very well to the idea. But his own dressing-room he had made pleasant, it was warm with brilliant lighting, and a long mirrored side to it, giving the impression of lots of room. He was sitting there in his shirt-sleeves, with his dresser wiping off the make-up.

She had never thought that backstage could be so ordinary, comparing oddly with the plush seating of the theatre, the quiet carpets, and the air of indolence, of wealth, and of extravagance.

The dressing-table was crammed with

tubes of make-up, and the dresser was a funny little man, almost a dwarf, hardly up to the top of Robin's head when he was sitting in his chair.

'I hope you liked it,' Robin said.

'I thought it was wonderful, and how on earth did you remember that long part?'

'Oh, one gets used to that, years of practice, and there is always the prompter.' His dresser helped him into his waistcoat and coat, and he accepted this without a word. The whole atmosphere of the dressing-room was entirely different from what she had anticipated, and somehow she found it practically impossible to associate this man with the one she had met on Tennyson Downs and with whom she had talked so gaily. In the theatre he seemed to her to have become the part he played.

'I know,' Robin told her. 'That has to be so. If I don't become somebody else, then I am no actor.'

It was one of those careers which she herself could never have followed, and she knew it. Her life was cut to pattern, his was a world of pretence which never came near reality. Hers *was* reality, one worked with death for ever standing in the background, an ever-present stranger waiting his turn.

She sat with him until he was ready, and

then they went out of the theatre together. He knew the restaurant to go to, one he liked, only just round the corner. She heard the sound of music before she got inside, all the tables grouped round the central dance floor, the band now rendering 'Alexander's Ragtime Band'. Ragtime had come into the world with the American Army, so it seemed, and with it all sorts of changes in dancing. She had been brought up on the polka and the waltz. Now it was ragtime.

They dined at a small table set on the edge of the dance floor, reserved for them, and three autograph books were waiting for him to sign. It was quite a different world, one which she had never thought about, but which she loved, and she found herself changing with it.

'It's lovely!' she said.

The weekend on the island had helped her, and tomorrow she would be in practice again, the telephone ringing, or so she hoped, and going visiting with all the old worries. But for now she would enjoy herself.

'What are you thinking about?' he asked her.

'Tomorrow,' she said.

'Don't forget that tomorrow never comes! It is always today,' and Robin smiled with his most fascinating smile.

She shook her head. 'Oh, tomorrow will come all right, and I shall be back seeing people who are worried to death about themselves, or I'll be going the rounds. It is fairly hard work, of course, but my need is to get sufficient patients to make good and earn my living. Difficult now that the two good men who joined up when the war came are back in competition.'

He nodded. 'Why did you want to become a doctor? To me it seems an odd idea for a woman.'

She wondered if she dared tell him the truth, and she hesitated for a moment. Then she said, 'I suppose it was because the actual saving of life always gave me a thrill. That is why I prefer surgery, one feels one is doing so much more. I have always wanted to fight to help people to get well again. Sometimes they won't let me help them to get well, they just don't try, and then I get worried about them.'

They compared their careers; his mission was to divert people's minds from their own troubles, and for a while to let them live in a new world, and an interesting one. Hers was to save life. They had some champagne, and he became more animated. She realized that he had been tired when he left the theatre;

apparently acting took it out of one, though he did not say so.

He said, 'Let's dance? You have spent your life in studying too hard. Now I have never passed an **exam** in my life, failed in the lot. I just pushed my way in. I think you have had far too much work and worry, and working in a small town laying the foundation stones of a practice that you did not buy must have been pretty tough.'

'It *was* tough, but I'll stick to it,' she said.

They danced, and that was an experience, for he was very good at it.

In this weekend she had found a new angle on life, and tonight she had to realize that this was goodbye. She was going back to her practice, to the waiting for calls, and the anxiety lest she would never get sufficient patients, and the full routine of her job.

Robin danced beautifully, and it was one of those wonderful floors on which one never tires. The band came from the States, and was an exciting one, she had never danced to music like this before. Tonight it seemed to be a hundred years since she had walked with him on Tennyson Downs, and quite a long time since the morning when she had driven up to London in his car with him. Tomorrow was already born, and tomorrow meant the end of a dream, and the return to reality.

He took her back to the hotel.

'It's been lovely meeting you, and you're going to have a surprise, for one of these Sundays I shall come down and see how you are getting on!'

She slept well, to be awakened by the chambermaid, who had been instructed to call her, for she had a train to catch. She had to force the breakfast down her throat, for somehow she did not feel like it (perhaps for the first time in her life), and she took a taxi to the station. Now, once she had started, she knew that every throb of the train sent the experience of the most wonderful weekend of her life into the distance. He had gone his way, and she was going hers, back to the job. The lovely weekend was just a memory to be laid by, but remembered for ever. She would never forget the light breeze and the warm sun on Tennyson Downs, the beautiful turf, and the feeling that this was something exceptional, something entirely different, unique, and it could never be repeated.

She had to take one of the shocking old 'flies' which hung about the home station, waiting for hire. They were a dying institution, of course, with the coming of the motorcar, and possibly horses of the kind that drew them would become extinct. She walked into her own house, and saw a pile of notes lying on the hall tray, and almost instantly the telephone rang.

'This *is* reality,' she told herself as she dealt with it.

Miss Willis came into the hall to welcome her. She was a great comfort, and Anna could not think what she would do without her. There was one telephone message from a rather nice young widow, in a street that was to hand. Her little girl had fallen down the stairs, and the mother thought that she had broken her leg.

'I will go round there now.' Anna said.

'The message only came two minutes back, and I told her you would be in at any moment. She seemed to be quite a lot upset.'

Anna went straight round.

Within a few moments she was in the house, and realized that this *was* a broken leg and the child must go to hospital. She sent a message for the ambulance. The mother did not want to part with the little girl, but for the time being this would have to be. Anna sent the mother along with her, set the leg in hospital, and got the child more or less out of pain.

She was back in her consulting-room

within a matter of minutes, or so it seemed. Miss Willis told her that at Weston it had been a somewhat raw rough Easter, and there was a lot of sickness going the rounds. Anna had never thought that it would accumulate as much as it had done, and all that afternoon it was a case of calls and visits that she had to pay on patients who had waited for her return. Suddenly a big barrier of work stood between herself and the time she had spent away from home. Then she had been a young girl enjoying her first sense of freedom after exams and difficulties. Now she was back as a doctor, surprised to have so many visits to pay, but things had mounted up. She had to give all she had to every visit as it came, and this could not be avoided. The whole future of her practice depended not on her high degree, or her good medicine, but on the fact that people liked her sympathy and understanding.

The holiday had done her good, it had been one of the most remarkable changes in her life, but it was over now. She had to thrust it aside as a beautiful dream which dies with the morning. But now her practice had caught up with her, she was even called out just as she was preparing for bed. Apparently some man had tried to commit suicide, and his terrified wife had sent her seven-year-old daughter to get the doctor. She went down to answer the door herself.

'What is it?' she asked.

In a matter-of-fact voice the child said, 'Me dad's tried to kill hisself.'

'I'll come,' Anna said calmly.

That was one of those hours when she really had to keep her head, for the thought of the coroner alarmed her very much indeed. Perhaps there had been something in it when, as a child, she had told her father that she wanted to be a doctor, and he had said that it could be hard going, but always worth it. She got the man round (he had not been very good at the job), but there was a lot of blood about, and that always worries the relatives a great deal. She managed to stitch up, and thought he was in no danger. A sleeping draught would give him a night's rest, and she consoled the wife, who came down to the door with her, just as the church clock struck one. There is a bit of a difference between tonight and last night, she thought as they stood there.

'Thank you for everything you did,' said the woman. 'I always says that women understand better than what men does.'

Anna knew that this was a very great compliment, and she had made a friend.

She said, 'Now you have a good cry if you think it will help you, and don't try to bottle it up! He is going to be all right, and that is the thing that matters most to both of us. I'll have a talk with him when he is better. Do try not to worry.'

She went back home feeling rather tired. She had thought that the lovely holiday in the island would have stopped this sense of deflation which came at the end of the day, but fighting death is an emotional strain, and she realized that it took a lot out of her.

She was called out again during the night, at three in the morning, which is the most ungodly time. It was a child teething and in convulsions, but she got him round and instructed the mother as to what to do if he had another attack. In the end she gave the directions to the father, who was a young bank clerk, for he seemed to be the more reliable. The mother was just exhausted with sheer anxiety.

Now the holiday had receded into the distance, and it seemed to be a long way off. But she had to remember that at any moment death himself could ring the bell for her to be out again.

'Forget the holiday,' she told herself.

It was difficult to get back into the routine,

although she had been away for only five days, but five whole days can make a tremendous difference to one's life when one comes to look at it.

There was such a lot of illness about, and she blamed Easter for most of it. Too many people in the world *will* look at Easter as being the start of the summer, which it certainly is not. Usually the bright sunshine is followed by sleety showers and a foul east wind which has a spot of pneumonia in it to surprise its victims.

CHAPTER FOUR

That was a stiff week for her.

On the Saturday, when things were a little slacker, she went over to the isolated village where Hugh Felton was the clergyman. When she thought about it, perhaps she should have done this before, but he had got on so well and had been such a good patient that she had trusted him. He had been out of hospital for three weeks now, and had told her that a parson friend was staying with him to do the visiting and take the services while he himself could not do it. She had explained that it was downright essential for him to take life easily for the first few weeks, on which his whole future rested. He must give the operation a chance to settle.

Her last warning to him in hospital had been, 'Now do go carefully, for this is so important. It never pays to get well too quickly, always give it a chance, and do remember that I am again warning you to go very slowly at first.'

He had promised, and she trusted him implicitly.

She drove through the village on one of

those glorious days which some people call 'weather-breeders', believing that because they are too good to last they will hatch out bad weather. Here there was every sign of the advancement of spring itself. A budding wood, with a pale yellow carpet of primroses in the grass. The willow trees were well forward with their light branches flecked with green buds opening in the amiable sun. 'How wonderful the country can be!' she told herself, and now wondered how she had ever come to waste the years in training in one of the grimmer, rougher parts of London, where one never saw these lovely things, nor could even guess what time of year it was.

She drove down the lane, with the red-roofed farm on her left, and all those clucking hens waiting to be fed, and the old forge on the hill, black and white (it had been there for generations). She turned in at the wide open gate which always looked as if it welcomed people, and that was what Hugh Felton had wanted of it. A rectory should be like home for everybody, he had once said to her.

Then she saw Hugh Felton himself crouching on all fours beside a small bed of flowers, and doing some most vigorous weeding there.

'And I did warn him not to rush things, or do anything like this,' she told herself with some horror. She stopped the car and got out of it, going across the lawn very quietly to where he was working. He seemed to be surprised when he turned and saw her approaching him.

'I thought you were away,' he said.

'It rather looks like it! Now I did tell you not to use that leg too much for some weeks, and here you are hard at it,' she said.

'I was only on all fours,' he said, and she had to laugh.

Then she said, 'Now we'll go inside, and you won't do it again.'

He explained that apparently he had become deeply interested in getting this particular bed finished, for it looked so awful from the house that it worried him. He tottered up looking rather like a naughty schoolboy who has been caught making paper darts in class.

'You did promise me,' she said.

'Yes, I know, but the place looked so downright awful that I could stand it no longer. I am proud of my garden.'

'I want to be proud of helping your leg to get well, and you are *not* helping that.'

He nodded.

'Somebody had to do something,' he said. 'The old man who usually does it became ill, and the new fellow is lazy as they come, and spends half the time at the pub, so I had a whack! I don't get half as tired as I did, and it *is* spring, and the sap is rising.'

He said it with a giggle, perhaps in the hope of talking her round, but she was not in the mood. There are in the world only two sorts of patients. There are those who make the most of everything and don't try to hasten their convalescence, for they enjoy being looked after. Hugh Felton was not one of these, he was one of those people who want to get well too quickly.

She said, 'You don't realize how much you are tiring yourself, but it was a long operation and there was a lot of pain after it. If it is to turn out to be a success, this part of the business depends on you, and grovelling down on the grass weeding flower-beds is *not* the right thing to do.'

'Oh dear!' he said.

They went into the house together, the bright sun streaming down, and she knew by the way he flopped down into a chair that he had worn himself out, but wouldn't say so.

'You see, you *are* tired, even if you try to hide it from me,' she told him.

He now admitted that he was. But in the spring everything grew like mad, and even with a gardener it was difficult to keep pace with it; somebody had to do something. Yes, he *was* tired, but the place looked so awful that one hated even to look out of the window. The pensioner would be back next week, which would be something, though not everything, for rectory gardens take some coping with, and it was very large.

'Your first duty is to make the effort to help yourself,' she said, 'and if only you let the garden go weedy for the next week or so you should stand a splendid chance of never having any further trouble. But you simply can't go about kneeling on damp grass and weeding.'

'I did have a hassock,' he pleaded. 'It was an old one from the church, but it must have been better than nothing.'

He ordered some tea for her, and he really was a very charming, kind and considerate man. It was pleasant to sit here and drink tea with him. He had a childhood very much the same as hers had been, and this was a common bond between them. He was an only child who had loved his home life, as she had done. And both of them had been spoilt by their parents. He confessed that the parental tenderness had scarcely prepared him for the hardships and the insistence of this grim world. But all his life he had wanted above all things to help others. He had come from a clerical family, most of his people had been parsons, and somehow with the profession running in the family the time comes when you are, as he put it, 'almost born in a dog-collar'. He hoped that she had had a nice holiday, for she needed it, and she glossed over it.

The tea was delightful, and she enjoyed it. He was one of those men to whom you could talk, and he understood everything that you wanted to say. He was rather like a young boy in a way, and youthfulness had stayed with him in a most attractive manner.

He was dedicated to his parishioners, and he very much wanted to improve their conditions. The previous rector had been slack about this, one of those men who live the life of a country gentleman and never exert themselves too much. She laughed at the description of him. But he was worried as to which way the world would go now that we had won the war.

It was going to be extremely difficult for working men who had become officers during the hostilities, to go back to being farm labourers and that sort of thing. Is there any real going back in life? That very question made her anxious, for everyone believed that we had won the war which was to end wars, after which there could never be another, and we should all live happily ever after. The war lay behind us, it could never recur, so she felt, and surely that was true? She changed the subject.

'This leg of yours,' she said. 'I never believe in misleading a patient, and I do speak the truth. There must be no gardening, no playing tricks with it, just rest it and give it a chance.'

He promised once again, and she thought she had got the message home this time. She only hoped that the moment she left he would not go back to finish off the flower-bed. But she didn't think he would.

She drove home along a lane bursting into vivid spring. The thick chestnut buds were casting aside their sticky brown overcoats, and here and there a bush of blackthorn seemed to be sparkling with a springtime snow. The hawthorns had that bright illusion of newly breaking leaves, and soon there would be the sharp white frost of riotous blossom of the may itself, in garlands!

When she walked into her own home there was a call from Lady Esmay, who was 'a bit worried about Alison again'. She spoke hurriedly as she always did when she got over-concerned; the child had had a bad cold and was not recovering as she should do. Anna glanced at the clock and realized that she would just have time to visit her and make her feel happier, then get back for evening surgery. 'I'll come round right now,' she said.

The big house lay on the far side of the town, standing in a large park, with the heavily budded chestnuts in an avenue which wound its way down to the house itself in the dell. The butler opened the door to her, and she went inside. It was a very beautiful country house, part of it two centuries old, and little did she think that we were coming to a period in the history of England when this sort of house could no longer stay as a private residence. Their day was closing in on us with the end of the horrific war, and ahead of us was little that was promising to be prosperous.

Anna knew that Lady Esmay was horribly alone in life, and she felt that the house was too big, too empty of friends and companions, and she badly needed help, though she would not admit this.

They sat down with the log fire in the huge grate, for it was quite chilly. The house echoed with the sound of footsteps on polished floors; the panelling was exquisite, and the view of the distant lake enchanted her, and there in the early summer the pink water lilies were amazing, so she had been told.

It was a magnificent home, though far too big for a lone woman whose husband had deserted her and the one child. Anna waited for Lady Esmay to tell her the trouble.

'It's Alison,' she said. 'She just cannot shake off her cold, and I dread the fact that the influenza could return.'

'There's no earthly reason why it should.'

'I know, but she went out to pick some primroses for me and when she came back she was coughing a lot. I was very worried when I heard her.'

It was over-anxiety, of course, but that in itself could be a disease. The poor woman was wretchedly nervous, as Anna knew, and possibly she was one of those people who, if they cannot find a worry, invent one. She had never got over the fact that her husband had absconded with another woman.

Anna went up to the child's nursery, to find that her chest was all right. She had a cough, of course, but most children had at this time of year, and there was nothing about which to be anxious. But she did feel that something ought to be done, not so much for the little girl as for the mother, and this was probably one of those cases when a woman doctor was far better able to cope than a man.

She went downstairs.

'She really isn't too bad, and I should have said that she was doing well. The English spring is always tricky, and we have been having what Shakespeare called "the blackthorn winter",' and then she brought out the idea that she had been brewing all the way downstairs. 'I suggest you take her down to the Riviera or somewhere like that for three weeks or a month, just to end the winter there.'

'Well, I suppose we could do it.' She did not turn it down immediately. 'But wouldn't the journey be too much strain for her after she has been so ill?'

'Not if you take it easily, and the climate would help both of you to feel better. It is almost summer down there now.'

'I know, but the trouble is that I don't want to take her away from *you*! I ... Oh, I daresay I am being silly, but I rely on you to help me through! I ... I'd be lost without you,' and her voice was tremulous.

Gently Anna spoke to her. 'Now look here, there is no sign of your needing me to help you through, as you put it. Alison had got over the influenza, and is better, but she wants building up. So do you! This would get you through the uncertain April weather, and you could stay there until something like summer starts here.'

She looked round the Oak Room in which they were sitting, and knew that it must be associated with a thousand memories of Lady Esmay's married life, and every one of them could hurt her. The poor woman was a worrier, and it had been intensified by everything that she had had to endure.

'But what should I do if she got influenza out there, and I was left with no one to lean on?'

Anna spoke calmly. 'I have a doctor friend near Cannes, whom I could trust, and so should you. I will write to him if you go, and I do want you to. You have had your fair share of worry in this house, and although possibly you don't realize it, it is the wrong background for you now. Do rely on my judgment. You are needing a change so badly.'

'But the risk of being away from *you* is what worries me.'

Anna tired to reassure her. 'I am quite an ordinary doctor, but I happen to have got your confidence. I can assure you there is this excellent man whom *I* would trust, and if I could, so should you. It is bad for you to rely on me too much.'

She contrived to talk Lady Esmay into it, and then went home late for her consulting hour. Four people were already sitting there waiting for her, and as she finished with the last man (who was a chatterbox) there came a telephone message for her from Dr Higgs next door. He was one of those men whom, although she had tried hard to like him, Anna could not stand. She regretted that she did not feel better about him, for it did not make life easier, and being dubious of an immediate neighbour was hardly pleasant.

Dr Higgs had tried to get hold of her at Easter, only to find that she was away. Could he see her?

Anna wished that she was not suspicious of him, but she always felt that he in his turn was suspicious of her, and she certainly did not care for him. Ever since his last partner had died, their practice had gone down rather badly. The new young man was not popular and, of course, his habit of visiting the public houses had caused a great deal of gossip in the little country town.

Anna was now wondering what on earth Dr Higgs could be wanting from her, and only hoped that this was not going to be something difficult. Could she come round? Or should he visit her? She thought that the latter might be the better. He arrived soon after. He came into her very pleasant sitting-room, where she had tea waiting for him.

He had been rather surprised when he had learnt that she had gone away for Easter. She gave him no indication of where she had been, realizing that this was what he wanted to know, or of what she had done. She was feeling even more anxious about this visit, even if the doctor had said that it was 'only a small matter' and would take only a few minutes. He was amiable, saying that he thought things had worked out very well, and how lucky they were to have an FRCS in their midst.

She did not warm to that!

'Thank you,' was all she said.

He did not manage to thaw her, she knew that somehow there was a lot more behind this. He purred on. She had done wonders for Lord Porth's son, undoubtedly the child would have died if she had not insisted on operating when she did. Then with Lady Esmay's little girl, and he had heard that they might be going to the south of France. She thought it was miraculous how these doctors managed to pick up stray bits of news almost before they had happened. There *must* be something behind all this, which made him so nice about everything.

Then they came to it.

He went on, gradually arriving at his point. It was quite ridiculous for them to be living next door to each other, and he now short of one partner, and she not in partnership with anyone. It had been Dr Webb who had been doubtful and had upset the idea. Then his own wretched nephew qualifying most unexpectedly at that very moment had brought things to a head.

She was aloof and cold, and he must have realized this, because he became more plain-spoken.

He admitted that he personally was none too happy with his late partner's nephew, but everything had been signed, sealed and delivered, and there was very little he could do about it now. What he wished was what he had always wished, so he protested, though she was very doubtful on this score. He had wanted her as third partner in the practice, that day when she visited them both, and, if she remembered, he had said so at the time. If he *had* said so, he had not insisted later on when the old man had written to her. He now said that he felt that the nephew had qualified at the wrong moment, and he laid all his cards on the table. He was now a very amiable old man, trying to persuade her into the partnership which had been refused to her when she had wanted it so much. From what she had already seen of the lazy young doctor's work, she had no wish to be allied with him in any way.

She said, 'I did hope that I made it clear the first time I came here that it was then or never. I bought the house and I had no choice but to go on on my own.'

Obviously he had not anticipated this, for instantly he was self-defensive. 'You put up your plate,' he said coldly.

'Exactly! And that plate is staying up!' She said it in a voice that she hardly recognized, but she did so dislike this man. 'From our conversation both you and Dr Webb gave me the idea that I should be helpful to you. I believed that I was to be the third partner.'

'We heard that young Dr Webb had qualified. We heard that very night, and, of course, being one of the family, he had to have preference.'

'Not entirely fair on me, when I had bought the house, almost on your suggestion,' she said.

He looked at her in a slightly bemused

manner, and she felt that she had made him unsure of himself. He was, she knew, a bad-tempered old man, who could be most unpleasant when annoyed, and she did not want this to become a row.

He said, 'You thrust your way into this place! You just set up your plate, and if that is good medicine you surprise me!'

She rose with dignity, and opened the door. She said, 'It would be a mistake to argue, and in this manner. You have a partner already, I thank you for thinking of me as another, but I prefer to keep things as they are.'

She knew that if looks could have killed she would have died where she stood, but she *had* to end the conversation. She thought that he looked considerably older than before, a trifle wizened. Changed.

He said, 'Very well, but remember, I shall not make this offer again.'

Perhaps she knew then that she had nothing to fear from his competition. The small town had clung to the very old doctor, but they had never liked his partner, and now actively disliked the nephew! She had by this time realized that she would be able to keep a practice here, and probably it would increase. She had been scared that when the two good doctors returned, she would be set back, but somehow that apprehension was fading. She walked with the old doctor down the hall, and put out a hand to help him into his coat.

'Let me help you,' she said.

'No, thanks.' He said it in a spiteful way, as if he resented everything she said or did. Not for the world would she have gone into practice with him, and now she recognized that the fact that those two doctors had turned her down was no tragedy, as she had believed last year, but a help! So often these things happen for the best. As he was so rude, she left him to cope with the special lock she had had put on her front door when she had found that a man in the town knew how to work the old one and was discovered in her hall at midnight. She asked Miss Willis to help him.

'I don't think he can get out. Can you get rid of him for me?'

'So that's it, is it?' said Miss Willis, 'and serve him right! I'll go along.'

Later, Anna heard the door close on him.

She knew that she had done the right thing, for however worried she got in black moments, she was beginning to find her feet here, as her mother would have put it. If she had not been doing well, Dr Higgs would never have wanted her to enter the partnership with him and his late partner's nephew. She *had* done the right thing.

She sat down in the sitting-room and she tried to pull herself together. She prayed that she had not been rude, for of course *he* had. By nature he was a rude man, and she knew quite well that the late doctor's nephew was a stupid lazy young man who would be no help to him. He had had what could have been a last-minute hope for filling in the blank. He had expected to get her into the practice in order to save it, and this was exactly what she was not prepared to do.

'Well, that is *that!*' she told herself.

CHAPTER FIVE

Anna felt that the lovely break that she had had, the long weekend on the Isle of Wight, had done her far more good than she would have imagined possible. She felt that she had grown years younger, perhaps because she had found a new self within her. It had been meeting Robin Grant, and suddenly throwing aside the practice, the long exams, the pressure of hospital work and everything that it entailed, for she had worked hard to get through those exams, and the FRCS had undoubtedly taken a very great deal out of her.

She came to the conclusion that on the whole she had done remarkably well, because the town had been stuck for a good doctor in their midst, having been saddled with the two old doctors Webb and Higgs, the one who came out on a bicycle, and the man who was never sober, and who had figured badly at a couple of inquests.

It was rather extraordinary how some men managed to carry on, when one came to think about it.

She had done well whilst the two other doctors were away with the army, and had established herself before they returned. Probably the little town had been wanting help all through the war years, and had been unable to get it. Now she felt strangely younger. She was not sure if it had begun with that walk on the downs, or because of the fact that she had needed the holiday so much.

On the whole she had found that the mothers of children preferred a woman doctor to a man, even if it was unusual. She hoped that she was kind, solicitous and helpful.

Her work with the Porth boy and with little Alison Esmay had travelled around. She could see that old Dr Higgs would have done well if he could have persuaded her to join the partnership, but she did not care for him, she thought that he had behaved very badly in the beginning. She allowed herself to be quite pleased that the nephew was such a hopeless man to have in the practice.

Anna had originally met the nephew when she had gone to visit a child suffering from polio in a village four miles away. He was coming out of the house next door just as she went up the path, and he spoke to her over the privet hedge.

'These are pretty ghastly villages,' he said.

He was a very ordinary man, much after

the pattern of the other two; she knew exactly what he would be like when he aged. They had a talk.

She didn't care for his hospital, the one in which his uncle had been trained, and he admitted he had gone in for the job not because he liked it, but as a means of making money, and he had his uncle's practice to step into. If he could pass, he added, and that had been hell!

She knew how many times he had failed in his finals; Miss Willis (who was the town chatterbox from whom nothing could be kept secret) had found this out and had echoed it around. What a woman she was for talking!

'I rather like villages,' she told him.

'Not my idea at all! In fact I find the whole thing a bit of a bore. No life here. Just drooling along, but it was a ready-made practice for me, so of course I stepped into it!'

She remembered that he had stepped into it just when she thought that she herself had done this. She disliked his manner, but she tried to be amiable.

'I love the work,' she said.

'Good Lord!' and then he added, 'I like London, lots to do and see. This mucky little town is ghastly. Dead as the dodo, and I find it dull. The awful thing is that I believe I am stuck here for life, God help me!'

'Something might happen, you never know,' she suggested.

He went down the path the other side of the privet hedge and got into his car with a scowl, and she went on up the path to see her patient.

She thought it a pity that he had so little enthusiasm, for this would not make things easier for him. But she had to remember that as far as medical etiquette went she had started off on the wrong foot, and this was something that she must not forget. Not that *he* was likely to let that happen! She could afford to smile as she thought of it.

The town was settling down to the post-war world. She now found that she need not have dreaded the return of the two younger doctors, for they were both very friendly men and easy to work with. Perhaps her load had been a trifle heavy, for she had had to do a great deal, but now she was in a far more comfortable position.

It was a fine serene day. She got into her car and drove out to see a couple of cases, and when she returned there was a telephone call from Dr Adams; he was the man with four children, and the nice wife whom she had met and liked. His baby son was not well, could she come round? She went at once.

It was a large old-fashioned house, such as abounded in the neighbourhood, furnished very comfortably, and she was taken up to the night nursery. The baby was in his cot with croup. It had been the cold spell in the last week that had done it, she told herself; she ordered him the usual remedies, and then had some coffee with the pleasant Mrs Adams, who seemed to be as friendly as her husband.

It was strange that she had rather dreaded the return of these two capable men, and one of the first things that had happened had been that she was called in to see after the baby son. They were kind people, and they told her that she had been saved a lot by not joining up with the two old doctors, and sooner or later they felt that something would happen with that nephew of the old man's. He hated the place, was not a good doctor, was not interested in the job, and spent too much time pub-crawling round the town.

She drove the car home. She had the feeling that she was now properly established. She had fitted in, which she had always been afraid might have been prevented by the fact that she had put up her plate. 'I did the right thing,' she told herself again.

CHAPTER SIX

In the first few months of peace, the houses brightened, and new coats of paint did a lot to change the shabbiness of the war-ridden world. Most of the young men coming out of the army bought motor-cycles with their gratuities, and there were eternal accidents. She had never thought that she could have so many broken legs and arms. Already the unhappy memories of the war itself were receding, and now dancing was the vogue. Even in this small dull town, everybody danced.

A local hotel had a dinner-dance every Saturday night, and it was the era of 'Hitchykoo' and 'Oh, you Beautiful Doll'. There *was* something about ragtime, and Anna had to admit that the tunes lingered in your head, so that she found herself humming them as she went from patient to patient.

It was a glorious spring, the first spring of peace, and she had never been more glad to see it. The practice increased, she was accepted by the two new doctors, and the Matron of the hospital was a real friend.

On the very hot Whit Sunday something happened. She had had a difficult week, for there had been a bad fire at a country farm, and two children had been cruelly burnt. Brought to hospital under her care, she had got them through the worst, and was sitting back at home for a little rest. Being Whitsun, most people had gone away, but as she finished her meal she heard the doorbell ring.

As Miss Willis went to open the door, Anna said through the door, which was ajar, 'Say that I am dead!' then heard the sound of a man's voice in argument. She would never know why she went out into the hall, but she did. The sunshine flooded through the door, and she instantly recognized the man as being Robin Grant. She nearly dropped down with surprise.

'Good heavens, *you*!' she gasped.

He came straight into the hall, almost pushing Miss Willis to one side (she said 'Tst! Tst!', her usual remark when affronted). He walked down the hall, and for some absurd reason Anna was glad that there were sprays of guelder-roses on the table, and peonies (Miss Willis, of course), and that sense of friendliness about the place which always seemed to pervade this house.

'Heavens, *you*!' she gasped again.

He was enchanted to be here, and he radiated the enthusiasm of a schoolboy who has a day off from school to which he is not really entitled. 'So I've found you!' and he chuckled.

'I thought you were a patient.'

'I've been very patient, if you ask me, and I can tell you that I am hale and hearty. There is nothing much wrong with me. I've come down for the day to take you out somewhere. Where shall we go?'

She said, 'Steady! I've only just come off duty and had my lunch. What about yours?'

'I had mine on the way. Now the world is our oyster! You've got a jolly nice place here, I must say. And you were having coffee?'

'Would you like some?'

They sat down and she poured out a cup for him. A guelder-rose was in full bloom beyond the window, with those greeny-white balls which it produces, almost like a summer snow of a strange variety.

'You *have* got a nice house,' he said.

'It attracted me to come here that autumn day when I first saw it, and instantly fell in love with it. Now everyone is wanting houses, and they will be double the price and still going up and up, all the time. Today I could get double for it, I know, but would not part with it for the world.'

'And the practice?'

She knew by the look in his eyes that he remembered that she had said Dr Higgs could be difficult. In a way his memory flattered her. She told him that she had been lucky here, for she had made friends in a remarkably short space of time.

'But of course you would.'

'I don't see why, for the world is not used to women in this job, though people are getting kinder. My surgery is of use, of course.'

She had never realized how glad she would be to see him again, and to talk freely of her work here; the suspense at first, and then finding the town opening up to her.

Robin, in his turn, had been up to his neck in cinematographic work. They were making a big film. He thought, with the war over, films were going to improve enormously. 'But the work is very tiring,' he said.

He asked to see all over the house, for he loved old places, and he thought that she had made a good bargain here, and she had bought it at the right time, also. Too many men had returned from the war and had gratuities to spend on buying a roof over their heads.

Then he said, 'Now what shall we do? It is such a lovely day and you are off-duty. Let's take the whole afternoon off and go out in my car and see places. It is a very beautiful part of England.'

'I'm free to go anywhere.'

They went out into the country, the chauffeur driving. They drove up into the hills, where there was real beauty, and little hamlets of black and white houses, with women standing and gossiping at their front doors. They had a pleasant tea, at a cottage which advertised that they provided teas, and there Robin was recognized, for the young daughter of the house had a picture postcard collection (then the rage) of famous actors and actresses, with the result that he had to put his name in her birthday book.

He had made plans to go back to dinner at the best hotel in Weston, which was not saying too much, but it would be a change.

Anna found herself intensely happy. The afternoon was like another lovely dream. This man had the trick of getting her away from her work. She knew that he had a very charming personality.

When they returned to the local hotel they found it most attractive. Old-fashioned in many ways, it provided good food, and they lingered over cold trout and a trifle, which were delicious. It was then, over the coffee, that he went back into the past.

'I never enjoyed an Easter more, and then bringing you up to London with me to see the play, and dancing afterwards.' He paused. 'I've entertained lots of people, but that was different. I . . . I have thought about you quite a lot, and wondered if you had forgotten me.'

'Of course not! To me that was like some sort of oasis in a desert. I had been most terribly worried about putting up my plate, and going through what was really a fight with the old doctors established here.'

'But they forced it on you. How could it matter so much? Anyone could put up a plate, surely?'

'Yes, perhaps, but it is *not* the thing to do.'

'You doctors worry too much about the right and wrong things to do. Those old men deserved it.'

'Yes, but I don't suppose they realized that, and now one of them is dead.'

'Well, good luck to the angels with him!' and he laughed.

He was working at the moment on a film, and his next booking with them was on Wednesday morning, almost at dawn, for they started absurdly early. He intended to spend that night in this local hotel, which surprised her.

'I am operating tomorrow morning, which is a bother,' she said, 'but I could give you a late lunch, about half-past one. Then we could do something in the afternoon.'

The curious thing was that when the afternoon came they just sat in the garden and talked. They compared their childhoods. He admitted that his parents had not been well off; she had been hard-up, fighting to scrape together the money to become a doctor as her father had been before her. Almost her last penny had gone in buying this house.

'But I got round that corner,' she said. 'God bless Eddie Porth's appendix! I had troubles originally, for the old men next door were dreadful, but now the two good doctors are back. I pray they don't take all the work from me,' and she made a grimace at the prospect.

They had finished tea in the garden when the telephone rang. It was a road accident, a doctor badly wanted, and the other doctors were out.

'I'll come,' she said, and took down the details, then turned to him. 'I'm sorry, but it is a road accident and I have got to go.' Already she had picked up her bag.

'You're quick on it!'

'But of course, a life could be at stake. Wait

here for me, and I'll be back the first moment I can.'

She was longer than she had expected, for a man was badly hurt, and she had to see him into hospital. When she got home, sad that the afternoon had been so interrupted—but this sort of thing happens in a doctor's life—she found that Robin was asleep in the easy chair.

She said, 'I am most awfully sorry, but I thought that the poor fellow was going to die.'

'And you return cool as a cucumber! Brave girl!'

'He ought to be all right now, but I was horrified at having to leave you alone for such a long time.'

He yawned and rose. 'It is all part of your job. I can't think why anybody ever *is* a doctor.'

She said, 'I do hope that you won't be stopped from coming down again because of this. It has been lovely seeing you. Next time make it my weekend off call,' and she said it in the tone that showed she really meant it.

This was one of those men who live in a world which was invented to entertain the public, but he took it very seriously, as she accepted the saving of life.

In the end he did not leave immediately, but decided that the later he went the faster he would be able to travel, for the early birds would jam the narrow roads.

She said again, 'It has been so nice seeing you. I am sorry that I had to be called out, but it is part of my life, and there is no way of avoiding it.'

'That's all right. I was with you for part of the time, and that was what I wanted. I could come down into the district in the summer for a ten-day holiday. You don't happen to know of a furnished house to let? I could bring servants with me, and it would be a big change.'

'It would be a big change for *me*,' and she did not like to admit how much the thought of it thrilled her. 'I will have a scout round. Do you mean a house here in the town, or in one of the villages round? Some of them are very pretty.'

He said that he preferred village life and would be delighted if she would do this. She knew that the idea was exciting. When he had gone she told herself that this was madness. She was perhaps passing through one of those girlhood phases which had come a little late. She was a doctor with a high degree, established now, in what was proving to be a good practice, and it was silly to fall for an actor who had, of course, hundreds of affairs in his life.

Then suddenly again she thought of the cool calm of Tennyson Downs, and the island. There he had seemed to be just a very charming man, though she had known that he was a famous actor.

I must pull myself together, she thought.

She had not been in bed ten minutes before she was called out by a young mother whose baby was arriving two months early.

She went off to the case, knowing that the mother was worried to death at the baby coming so early. The father was naturally distracted, and she should have been called before, for the baby arrived in the next quarter of an hour, a really lovely son.

They had badly wanted a son.

The young father was most helpful. As she finished she said, 'You ought to be a doctor, or a male nurse! If ever you run out of a job, get in touch with me,' and then, 'He really is a lovely little boy.' She would never outgrow the enthusiasm she always felt when she brought a living child into the world.

A neighbour came in to tidy up, and when she had got the young wife settled and the baby in his cot, she had a word with the husband.

'She'll be all right now, and the baby is as strong as you can get. He'll do well. Call me if you are in any trouble, but I think everything will be OK.'

She left them then, with the baby sound asleep and apparently quite all right. She promised that she would call again as soon as she started her rounds in the morning, and then she got into the car to return home and once more get to bed. It was still just the right side of midnight, the town was quiet, and as she drove slowly past the White Lion which was shutting up for the night, to her horror she saw that a man was lying motionless in the gutter, still as death, a mere hulk of a man.

She stopped the car and went to him, to find that it was young Dr Webb.

At first she had thought that he *was* dead, but now she discovered that he was breathing, though unconscious. He had been rather badly beaten up, and as she heard the sound of the locking up of the pub, she went into it. There was one somewhat unobliging barman there, and he looked at her.

'I'm Dr Thorpe,' she said, 'and there is a man lying unconscious in the gutter outside.'

He said, 'Yes, I know, we had to throw him out, he is one of the doctors, and he was drunk and making a row.' He accepted all this quite calmly.

'Yes, but he is hurt and I need help to get him into my car so that I can take him either home or to the hospital. I think he is badly hurt.'

The barman was most unhelpful, he was not the type of man with whom she had any sympathy. 'He was dead drunk and kicking up a hell of a row in here. Fighting drunk,' he told her, but he did come out into the street, though obviously reluctantly.

'The fact that he was drunk has nothing to do with it,' she said. 'I will take him back to Dr Higgs, or to hospital. Possibly hospital would be better. He is injured, badly so. You men should be more careful in what you do. Now give me a hand to get him into my car.'

When she was really angry she could be most compelling, and here in the starlight, with the small town quiet, and the disgruntled barman giving an unwilling hand, she felt strangely commanding. The man *was* hurt, and perhaps it would be better to go to Dr Higgs first, and ask if the young man should go into hospital, or if he wanted him at home.

The barman was glad to see her go, and she

went carefully, stopping outside the old doctor's. Apparently there they had gone to bed, and in the end Dr Higgs came down to answer the door for her, wearing the most ghastly dressing-gown of a plaid variety, something from the last century, she thought, and not cleaned for years.

'This is a nice time of night to knock people up, I must say!' he grunted when he saw who it was. 'What on earth is the matter?'

She told him that she had found the young doctor unconscious in the gutter, thrown out of the White Lion when they were locking up for the night. She thought he ought to go to hospital, for he looked to her to be really poorly.

The old man listened, still very angry, then he said 'Tst! Tst! Tst!' and she gathered from the way he accepted the situation that Dr Webb's nephew had always been something of a pest, who just went from pub to pub. She had heard this in the town, as one does, and from Miss Willis, but she always tried not to listen to local scandal.

'Shall I take him along to hospital? I have not examined him, but it might be the skull, and if so he will need care.'

'No, no, no, he has done this before. It's nothing much,' said the old man, all the time furiously angry that this had happened. 'Give me a hand with him indoors, and I will get him to bed.'

There were no thanks at all, he was not that sort of old man, and now there came the immense difficulty of getting the patient within. He was groaning a lot, and she was worried for him, but every time she suggested that he needed treatment, the old doctor shut her up. He attributed it to some form of drunkenness, and she knew the reputation the young man had, so of course Dr Higgs could be right.

The patient still groaned as they got him upstairs, and the doctor took every advantage of her youthful strength and her willingness to lend a hand. They got him into one of the most untidy small bedrooms that she had ever seen, and dumped him on to the bed.

She told the old man, 'You know, I am not at all happy about his condition, and he ought to be properly examined, immediately.'

The old man glared at her.

'He isn't your patient!' was what he said.

For a moment she was tempted to walk out and leave him to it, but she knew that the patient was in a bad way. How wise she had been never to come here as a partner if this was the sort of thing that happened!

'Well, if I can do no more, I leave him in your charge,' was what she said, 'but I should have liked to get him into the hospital, for *I* think he is badly hurt.'

The old man peered at her, in the way people do when they cannot see very well. He said, 'He is *not* your patient anyway, and I know him well enough to be aware of exactly what has happened. There has been a fight in the pub, and he got knocked out! This has happened before. He is all right. After all, I *am* a doctor, and I was a doctor before you were born, so suppose you leave my own partner to me, because I am perfectly capable of seeing after him.'

'Never a thank you,' she thought as she went down the stairs. The place was shabby, of course, but then when men run a house this often happens, and careless servants take advantage of the fact that they do not know what to do. She let herself out and went home to bed.

She was tired, overtired perhaps. It is strange in a doctor's practice how the work changes, sometimes easy going, then suddenly just the opposite. Eventually she did get to sleep, and Miss Willis woke her with the early morning cup of tea. Miss Willis knew everything that had happened, although she had been asleep at the time, for she was one of those women who scoop up local scandal and gossip.

'There has been ever such a nasty accident,' she said, 'and the paper boy tells me that the nephew of the old man next door was chucked out of a pub and fell down and broke his head.'

'What do you mean "broke his head"?'

'They do say that his skull was cracked. I heard the hospital ambulance come for him when I was getting up. I didn't see anything, but he went off in it, the paper boy says.'

Anna nodded. She said, '*I* took him home last night, picked him up out of the gutter and took him to Dr Higgs, who was not too pleased about it.'

On Miss Willis's face there was the expression which gave the idea that she was not surprised about that, and personally thought that the old doctor would have been no help to him. Anna had surmised this at the time. She knew, of course, that she ought to have taken the patient to the hospital, but he had smelt so strongly of alcohol that it could easily have been merely a drunken debauch, and she did not want to advertise that this sort of thing happened to a medical man practising in this small town.

She said nothing to Miss Willis, who was too much of a gossip anyway, but when she got downstairs she rang up the Matron of the hospital. Matron told her that the doctor had been brought in a couple of hours ago, and was now in the operating theatre with Mr Jack Scott operating on him. He had a fractured skull and was in quite a bad way. The Matron was not optimistic.

'I picked him up last night,' Anna told her, 'and I wanted to bring him along to hospital straight away, but Dr Higgs was adamant. I did not get a very pleasant reception, of course, so I handed him over to his partner, and after that everything lay in his hands.'

'Quite,' said the Matron, but she was none too encouraging, and although she did not give an opinion, Anna felt that she thought that things were fairly bad.

She attended to her own surgery with that calm which is part of a doctor's heritage. If the patient died, there would be an inquest, and she would have to give evidence, which she would be called upon to do. She felt now that she should have laid down the law in the beginning and have insisted that she took young Dr Webb straight to hospital, where anyway he would have been properly cared for. She was now ashamed that she had left him with his very angry and unwilling partner in a messy little back bedroom, where he was bundled on to the bed and probably left till the morning, as she thought now.

She finished with the morning surgery, and so far no real news had come from next door, so Miss Willis said, and if there was any news going about, Miss Willis was always the first person to get hold of it.

Anna could not keep on ringing up the hospital, which had a far too busy phone anyway, and she had had quite sufficient of Dr Higgs's rudeness when she had brought the poor fellow back last night. She knew that the old doctor had the habit of answering the telephone himself, and this was the last thing she wished for.

It was after lunch that the news came through, and by then it was running all through the town. They had got the doctor through the operation, and back into bed, but he had not recovered consciousness, and had died later. She gathered that it had been a terrific operation, a very serious one, for when they opened up, they had found other things, and undoubtedly in the White Lion the poor young man had been handled extremely roughly. Anna had loathed the barman and privately blamed him for most of it, though, of course, the young doctor was well known for being a troublesome customer. This was the most dreadful thing to have happened.

It would mean an inquest, and without any doubt—as she had taken him home—she would have to appear as a witness, which was quite the last thing that she wished to do. No doctor is particularly keen on inquests.

She should have taken him to hospital, not home, and could not think why she had been so silly. Undoubtedly he had been involved in something which she would have called a rough-house, and was badly hurt and needing help, but one would have thought that Dr Higgs would have realized this. She ought to have remembered his eternal tendency to cover up anything which he thought 'might lead to some unpleasantness', and of course he had been furiously angry, which she could well understand. Even more so because the woman doctor who had refused to join up with his practice when he asked her, should have been the one who had brought the young nephew back unconscious.

She knew now that she *should* have gone with him to the hospital last night, for his skull had been fractured, and Mr Jack Scott had operated. She telephoned him.

She said, 'I should have brought him in last

night, but Dr Higgs refused to let him go, said it was nothing, it had happened before, and now he is dead.'

Mr Scott, who was a most sympathetic man, said, 'You would not have saved him even if you had brought him in last night, so don't let that worry you. He was too far gone, there must have been the most dreadful fight, but the coroner will go into all that.'

'*The inquest*,' she thought in cold horror, 'and I shall have to be a witness, and I did the wrong thing.'

She was, of course, far too closely committed in the affair, and she felt most unhappy about it. Unfortunately she was the one who had found the man in the gutter, and had mistakenly taken him home.

She sent round a brief note to Dr Higgs, expressing sympathy and offering condolences, saying that if there was anything that she could do to help him, she would be only too willing to do it. But she received no reply of any sort. She thought that he must be considerably shaken, for apparently he had not even examined the young man, but had left him in bed to come round.

The affair haunted her for the rest of the day, and she felt herself deeply worried about it, it was a ghastly thing to have happened.

Later she realized that possibly nothing could have saved him. There had been a rowdy fight, and he was much too badly damaged; he was too far gone for anything to have saved him. If he had recovered, he would not have been *compos mentis* for the rest of his life. Perhaps it was for the best that he had gone.

'Now we wait and see what happens next,' she told herself.

CHAPTER SEVEN

The three days before the inquest seemed to occupy an eternity of time, Anna felt. The whole town was in a furore about what had happened, but there was one certain thing—although they pretended to be hopelessly shocked, they were thoroughly enjoying a good scandal!

Nobody had cared very much for the young man who had died so tragically, which possibly had been the reason why so many of the patients had transferred to Anna. She wished that she did not keep thinking of it with such apprehension, but she was very much upset by the incident. But he *had* been a nasty young man, doing the job merely to provide himself with an income, and he infinitely preferred a pub crawl to staying at home with Dr Higgs. Anna felt that he had something there, for she found Dr Higgs a terrible old bore.

On the morning of the inquest Anna went to the coroner's court with a sinking heart. One had to admit, of course, that this was a great day in the small town of Weston, the people were determined to get the most out of it. You could not have got a fly into the courtroom, it was so full. Already a most exaggerated story of the accident was going the rounds.

When Anna went into the witness box, she was deeply worried, for at all costs she would have to try as far as possible to keep Dr Higgs covered, though privately she gave him a considerable share of the blame. He had refused to diagnose the case, and would not let her do it when she had offered. He had insisted that the affair had been merely an ordinary bar fight, and it had happened more than once before this.

The coroner asked if she had done anything medically for the young man. She said that her first idea had been to get help to him at the hospital, but then she had felt that this decision should lie with Dr Higgs.

'He was in a bad condiition?' the coroner asked her.

'Yes, indeed he was.'

She had made the barman help her to lift the deceased into her car, because he was too heavy for her to manage alone. The coroner asked if she had examined him, and she said no, it would have been impossible in the street, and her one idea had been to get him home or to hospital, where a proper examination could be made.

She was asked what had happened when she got to Dr Higgs's house.

It was difficult not to disclose something that would be of disadvantage to him, for on looking back she realized that absolutely nothing whatever had been done. She replied that with the doctor's help she had got the young man into his bedroom.

Had she examined him then? the coroner asked her.

She explained that she had not. The deceased was Dr Higgs's partner and his patient, and he thought that he should be allowed to sleep it off. To her knowledge nobody had examined him, and she knew that things were getting more and more awkward. She could not very well say that Dr Higgs had been most averse to getting him into hospital, as he wanted the incident kept quiet.

'Dr Higgs is my senior,' she told the coroner, 'and I asked him what we ought to do. Personally I should have taken him to hospital, but Dr Higgs thought that he would be far better at home.'

It was very late at night, and she had realized that the old man was considerably disturbed.

'So nothing was done?' the coroner asked.

She said that there was a head wound, but she had not been allowed to examine the man. She had left him with Dr Higgs and had then gone home, so did not know what had been done. She said, 'I was not his doctor and I couldn't thrust myself forward. I had felt that my job was to take the young man home, and if the doctor wished it, then on to the hospital, but he did not wish this.'

She knew that the coroner was not pleased with her, and seeing what had happened, she was not particularly pleased with herself.

The coroner regarded her coldly. 'So you made no attempt to save the deceased's life?'

She was horrified, and resented this remark. 'In the presence of a doctor much older and more experienced than myself, naturally I stood back,' she said, and although her tone sounded deliberately cool, she was anything but cool deep inside her.

'And he died in the early morning?'

'So I understand. There seemed to be bad head injuries, but I had not the chance to diagnose a fractured skull, I could only have done so by a complicated examination, which I did not have the opportunity to make. Nor did I feel that I was the right person to make it.'

She stood down for Dr Higgs to go into the

box. He lost his temper with the coroner, and said a lot of silly things. He had apparently jumped to the conclusion that this had been one of those entirely usual bar fights, which had constantly happened in this young man's life. He had warned him about them before, and had done everything in his power to stop him from his stupid behaviour.

Dr Higgs agreed that his partner had been extremely drunk, and there was very little that could be done with an unconscious man.

Anna really was quite sorry for the old man standing there in the witness box and looking pathetically broken, and his hands were twitching with dismay. The coroner finally said that he thought it was most careless of the two doctors not to have discovered between them that there was a fracture, and to have made no attempt to assess the damage which had been done. If the real trouble had been discovered earlier, it could perhaps have saved his life. He deprecated what he called gross inefficiency.

From the first Anna had realized that the coroner did not like her, though really she had done nothing that was absolutely wrong. She had taken the young man to his partner to ask what she should do, and she did not think that she deserved any of the extremely nasty remarks that the coroner made about her.

From the first she had disliked the doctors next door, they had done absolutely nothing to help her. Now the coroner's remarks were the last straw, for she *had* tried to persuade Dr Higgs to let her take the young man to hospital, but he wanted to keep the whole thing dark. There had been sufficient gossip already about his drinking habits, and he did not want it to go further.

Apparently with the very early morning his moans had aroused the household and Dr Higgs had found that he really was most dangerously ill. Then he had acted, but it had been too late.

Anna left the court utterly dejected. It had been a horrible ordeal, and she did not know how she had managed to face it outwardly so calmly and complacently. She went home with a bad headache and was very much upset. Miss Willis turned up with aspirin and a cup of tea. She of course knew everything that had happened, so did everybody else in the town, and it would all be in the local newspaper, which was *not* what Anna wanted.

She felt that the eventual verdict of death by misadventure was a scar on her own self, she couldn't think why, for she considered that she had done all she could.

As time moved on she appreciated that it had been undoubtedly the greatest stroke of good fortune that this young man had not done it before, she wondered how he had lasted so long, seeing the fights he had had in local bars, for these were spoken of in court. He was, when in his cups, a very quarrelsome man.

The major trouble was that every one of her patients wished to sympathize, and it was very difficult for her to stand clear of it all, and not allude to it. Really, life for the time being became a worry to her, because everyone wished to talk of it, and she did *not* want it mentioned.

When she came to think about it, she considered that the young doctor had, in some ways, been fortunate for he had never recovered consciousness; had he done so, he would have been in intense pain, but he had slipped out of the world quite quietly. She did not attend the funeral; it was a busy day with many visits to make, and surely they could not expect her to neglect her patients?

That afternoon she went over to Hugh Felton's village to see how he was getting on, and she felt, as she always did, that there was something very comforting when she entered that large sprawling old rectory with the lovely garden surround. He came across the stone hall to greet her.

'How very nice to see you! And you are just in time for a cuppa.'

She was grateful to sit down in an easy chair, and to be here, for this place had a quiet reaction of its own, and she knew that she had always been susceptible to this.

The house was shabby, of course, for the stipend was so small, but it had this homely welcoming feeling which made her so happy. He was most kind, as he always was. He had walked remarkably well as he came across the hall to greet her. They talked about it. He felt that he could do more every day, but was still adhering to her advice and not rushing it. There came a slight warning ache when he did too much, and he trusted to this. She told him of the worry of that night when she had taken the young doctor back to his home and had left him there. Now she wondered if she had done the right thing, because the hospital would have operated earlier, and she kept telling herself that his life might have been saved, though the surgeon had denied this.

He said, 'I should not be sure of that. You did what you believed to be the right thing at the time. Probably he would have died whatever you had done. It is no good looking back into the past.'

She said, 'I did what I thought was wise, but he *ought* to have gone to hospital. Dr Higgs was terribly angry about it at the time, and was most unpleasant.'

'I hear he is retiring.'

She had heard that this was rumoured, but could not believe it was true. She could not think what he would do.

Hugh Felton said, 'I believe he is going back to his old home in Yorkshire. He came from that part of the world, and I think perhaps it is a good idea.'

She confessed, and it was something that she would never have dared to admit to anybody else, 'He was most unpleasant to me; we should never have got on well together, of course. I am always very thankful that I didn't join up with the firm, as I expected to do when I first came down here to see the old man, last autumn.'

Hugh Felton said, 'I think that the coroner was most unkind. A life was lost, chiefly through the young man drinking so heavily, and all he did was to rub salt into the wound.'

She had felt very badly about it all. But she had done her best at the time, and she had been at home when young Dr Webb had died. But she felt that the coroner had been particularly scathing to her because she was a woman, and most certainly he had made the most of that. She said, 'I did the wrong thing, but from what I heard of the post mortem, I doubt if he would have lived anyhow.'

Hugh Felton nodded. 'I think the wise thing is to forget it if you can,' he said. 'Whatever you did would have made no difference really. In a way it has cleared things up. It began with the old man dying, both of them were too old for the job, and if it had not been for the war they would have given up a long time ago. I feel that many more lives were lost in the war than those lost at the front, because of the awful conditions here at home. It seemed like that to me.'

'Maybe you are right,' she said.

They had their tea quietly sitting there in the big comfortable dining-room, with the view across the fields to the distant hills, and with that peace which somehow seems to make a rectory happy.

In the end he had to go, for there was a choir practice, and he was wanted at it. 'You see, I am the only person here who can play the harmonium,' he explained with a laugh.

She went back to her own home, for it would soon be time for her evening surgery. Miss Willis had got all the news. The old doctor was retiring, said she, going back to his home in Yorkshire, and then was rather disappointed that Anna already knew this. The house next door was to be sold, and much to her annoyance Miss Willis could not find out who was after it. Anna knew it would not be long before she got any information that she wanted, and by the end of the evening surgery she would probably know more.

When she thought about it, retirement was the only course left to Dr Higgs, and although she did not like the man, she felt that the coroner had been very plain-spoken about him. And about her. But time would make people forget and enable her to go on living life. The thing to do was to be as ordinary as possible, for every day in every life new events come along to crowd out the old.

Later on Anna learnt definitely that Dr Higgs was going right away, leaving the place for ever. It was almost immediately after that when Anna met Dr Graves, and he sympathized with her. He said, 'It's no good dwelling on it, coroners can be fairly merciless, and I very much doubt if anyone could have saved the poor fellow, for he had had a frightful blow. If they had got him round, I am sure he would never have been what he was before. Don't let it depress you too much.'

'I admit that it does worry me. I did nothing to help him, trusting to Dr Higgs. It really did rest with him. And then the young man died.'

The older doctor nodded. He had the power to console, this man with the quiet eyes and the most comforting manner. She told herself that the power to console was the one thing that a doctor needed most. He thought that it was quite time that the two very old doctors had gone. We stood on the threshold of a new world, the one that we had made by winning the world war.

'There is a new future ahead for all of us,' he said.

She was glad to see the two good doctors now in the town, for last winter she had been completely horrified at the indifferent medical men there were around. They were all well behind the times, but this was not by any means the only town which war had left bereft of good medical attention. When she had first come here she had in a way condemned herself for what she looked on as poaching on somebody else's practice, but Weston had been left with what Miss Willis called 'just the old duds', and she had not been too wrong.

'Now we look ahead,' she told herself.

*   *   *

One evening, with the very early summer already here, and wild roses budding in the hedgerows, Anna was called out to yet another road accident. It was on the road from London, and a large car had rounded a nasty corner going too close to the verge, where a stationary car had been standing in a highly dangerous position. There was an almighty crash, because the chauffeur had not seen the stationary car until it was too late to avoid the impact; apparently he was hurt, and the man sitting in the back was unconscious. Anna went along to see them. She drove cautiously round the corner, and realized that the local policeman was already there, a cumbersome, rather stupid man who would be no real help to anyone. The chauffeur had a black eye, coming up in a hideous shade of purple and blue, but barring a cut hand he was not as much hurt as she had imagined he would be when the accident had been reported to her. The man sitting in the back of the car was slumped down in the corner of the seat. She opened the rear door which had been badly damaged when hitting the other car, whose passengers had not been injured, as they were picnicking on the verge. Anna was told that the man did not seem to be hurt, but he had fainted and they couldn't get him round.

She spoke to them. 'I am a doctor, let me deal with him.'

Her voice seemed to rouse the man, for he turned his head to look at her, and to her utter amazement she saw that it was Robin Grant! He stared at her as if he had seen a ghost, rubbed his eyes hard, and then managed to blurt out, 'What the hell has been happening here?'

'There has been a slight collision,' she told him, 'and I was sent for to come along and see if there was anything I could do to help.'

He was still staring, and she knew that the crash had at first knocked him unconscious, but now he was coming round. She got into the car and came to the conclusion that it was merely shock, no more. He said that one wrist hurt him, but it was nothing very much, in fact it was astonishing that neither he nor the chauffeur had been badly hurt.

She asked him, 'What on earth are you doing coming down here?'

He grinned at that. 'I am supposed to be a surprise to you, and what is more, I seem to have come by express post, and to be a far bigger surprise to you than I had ever expected to be.'

'Are you making for the hotel?'

'Oh no.' He now seemed to be much more certain of himself and recovering very quickly. 'I have taken a furnished house in a little village called Burbage. It was offered to me by a fellow actor; it's close to you.'

She said, 'The chauffeur says the car is not so damaged that it can't go on. I suggest that I take you on in my car. I am glad that you are going to Burbage, for the parson there is one of my patients, and a great friend too. Now let's see if we can get you there.'

She had a word with the policeman who was laboriously writing down notes about the accident; the trouble with these village policemen was that they were always so slow, she told herself. He had got all the details he wanted, and thought it would be a good thing if she did take the gentleman to Burbage. The police would bring the chauffeur and the car along a little later, when the notes were all finished. The chauffeur had a very nasty black eye, but the policeman thought he would be all right.

She got into her own car, and turned it back to face the right direction. She went slowly because she felt that speed might worry him, and however well he felt, he had had a nasty shock, and she would be glad to see him resting and quiet in the furnished home. When they got to the village it was the old black and white forge, with low ceilings and lattice windows. Apparently it belonged to some people who had had it restored quite beautifully, and let it furnished on occasions. Robin's friend had taken it for the summer, and was lending it to him for odd weekends.

'I wanted to come here,' he said, 'as I knew it was close to you.'

She left the car and went up the steep rise to the forge itself. The door was wide open on to a flagged floor, and a sitting-room with latticed windows beyond. A village woman was setting a gate-legged table for a meal, and she turned sharply, instantly recognizing the doctor.

Anna explained what had happened.

They went up the crooked stairs to a bedroom with chintz curtains which had moss rosebuds on them, and somehow seemed to be part of the spirit of the place. She suggested that he should lie down for a short while. She could visit a baby who was sick in the village, while he rested, and would return later on to see how he was.

He said that he had a bad headache.

It was shock, of course, and possibly he had

hit his head hard, for he would have been flung forward with the impact, but all this would pass. If he could sleep he would feel better, and she left him on the bed.

It was a charming house, and the people who owned it had furnished it really well in accord with its period, so that it was a pleasure to be in it. She went off to see the sick baby, finding him much better, and the mother distinctly happier. It always presented a difficulty when a small child was ill, for anxiety weakened the mother and made her sick also. Anna stayed some little time, and then returned to the old forge where Robin was still resting.

He had slept and had wakened again, disturbed by a flock of sheep being moved from a pasture to a new field, but he felt better. She persuaded him to have some supper in bed, and then the chauffeur appeared, and she attended to his eye.

Both of them were very shaken, which time would make a great deal better. They needed rest and quiet, and this was free for all in the little village, with only the distant sound of lowing cattle, and the noise that the sheep made protesting at having been moved from one pasture to another.

She promised that she would come over

and dine with him tomorrow night, but now she must get back to her surgery. He might feel rather stiff in the morning, but she thought it would not be too bad. Before she finally left for her surgery, she went into the rectory to see Hugh Felton, and to ask him to keep an eye on things for her. He was surprised when he found her standing in the porch.

He said, 'Whatever are you doing here?' and then, 'Come in and have a bite of something?'

'No, I can't do that. There has been a minor accident on the main road, and I was called out to it. One of the people involved is Robin Grant.'

'Not the actor?'

'Yes, he *is* the actor. I know him slightly, and was most surprised to find him there. He was coming to the Old Forge for the weekend and on the way they ran into a stationary car at a blind corner on the London road. He is quite all right, except for a certain amount of shock, but the chauffeur has a very nasty black eye, and a cut on his hand. They were lucky to get away with it as easily as they did. Now I have to go back to my surgery. I do wish you would pop along to the forge and see if everything is all right.'

'Yes, of course I will. Fancy having him in the village! It is a very small world when you come to think about it.'

'Bless you,' she said. 'Now I really must go,' and she got into the car.

She had the feeling that somehow she was standing on the brink of a thrilling adventure. She had naturally been enchanted to see Robin, though at first distressed by the accident. As she drove back to her surgery, she thought of the tremendous difference in the history of the world that these last few months had made. The war was over, and they were never going to return to the old world and style of living, as they had once thought they would, but to a world that had completely altered.

It seemed that the old-time segregation of classes had gone for ever as a result of the war, in which a common impulse had combined everyone, and ploughboys had become colonels, and professional men had become privates. 'It is a very strange new world,' she said to herself, 'but probably we shall get used to it, and colonels will go back to being ploughboys,' though she really thought that this was highly unlikely. 'We shall all have to learn to live with the new world,' she told herself.

Robin Grant was better next day.

'And you'll dine here tonight?' he asked her.

He wanted this so much that she felt she could not refuse, and she arranged to go along after her surgery. He was still suffering slightly from shock, as she knew, and she felt that he needed somebody with him, a quiet meal, and a calm and relaxed evening which would probably do more for him than any medicine.

At the last moment, just as she was dressed, Dr Graves phoned her. From the first he had always been so kind to her, was an excellent surgeon, and she liked him very much. Could she operate for him in the morning? The patient preferred a woman to a man, and had said so. Could she just go round to the hospital where the patient now was, and introduce herself tonight, then it would be all right for the morning? She phoned Robin to say that she would be late.

When she got to the hospital, Mrs Harbourne was in one of the two private wards they had, and Anna recognized that she was a proper old martinet.

'So you're a doctor!' she said. 'Well, you don't look like one. I wanted to have a woman because men always rush you into all sorts of things that you don't want, and I won't be rushed.'

'You need never have anything that you don't want,' Anna said, 'but this operation ought to be done. Going on as you are only means increasing pain, and it should be done now.'

'Could it kill me?'

'The operation? *Most* unlikely. And I can promise you that after the first four hours you will be a lot more comfortable, and thankful that it has been done.'

The old lady looked quizzically at her. 'I wonder if I can trust you,' she said dubiously.

'Nothing like speaking your thoughts out loud!' Anna said to herself, and she replied, 'Lots of people have trusted me, and I don't think I have let them down. I am glad you are having it done, because I am sure it will help you.'

The old lady was still doubtful. 'It also helps the doctors,' she commented, 'they get paid for it.'

'If a doctor can save you pain, surely it is worth paying for? After all, it costs quite a lot to become a doctor, it is a very long training.' She smiled encouragement.

The old lady liked her, and agreed with her; in the end she arranged for the operation to be done. It would be next day, to avoid her changing her mind again, and they were lucky, for she had very little pain, and came out of the anaesthetic vowing that she would never have a male doctor again!

'I'm sorry about that,' Anna said to Richard Graves when she told him about it.

'Don't you worry! She'll have a row with you before very long, because she's like that. She changes her doctor as often as she changes her mind, and that is quite a lot of times.'

   *   *   *

Anna dined with Robin Grant at the Old Forge, and he had recovered very well. He was one of those men who are highly sensitive to shock, but he had said he would rest as she ordered only if she dined with him, so she did. She told herself that whatever an actor may say to the contrary, he lives on his nerves, and this makes things very difficult for him. She came back from seeing the old lady in hospital, and changed into a different dress to dine with Robin. It was a summer dress, with flowers on it. It was new and gay, and somehow she felt that the evening demanded this of her.

'I am going to enjoy myself,' she thought as she got into the car, 'even if I am a little late, but it has been one of those unfortunate things.'

It must be so pleasant to have something of an ordinary life. Although she had selected medicine of her own free will, at the same time she had never thought of the tremendous amount it would ask of her, and the long hours she would have to keep. One did not mind when a patient was desperately ill, but she did object to the complainers and the ones who only thought they were ill.

The hall door was wide open when she got there, and he came out to meet her. He looked radiant, and quite restored, but said that the chauffeur's hand was still hurting him a lot; could something be done for it? She did see the chauffeur; she had told him that it would be painful for a few days, but he was one of those people who liked being ill, and, as she said, 'If you had not gone round the corner so fast that you could not save yourself, your hand would have been all right today,' which did not make him like her any more, but it did serve him right.

The dinner was superb, for a good cook had come in from the village to help, and they ate it in the patio behind the house. The view beyond an apple orchard to the Cotswolds was delicious. And Robin had been told that on fine days one could see the outline of the Welsh mountains. He did not believe it, but people assured him that it was true.

There is a lovely contrast between a doctor's work in the theatre, and always dealing with people who are sick, and the sweet calm of an apple orchard, far hills, and the beautiful serenity of approaching night.

Then afterwards Robin asked her how she had got on at the inquest, and she admitted that she had hated every minute of it.

'It was really quite awful,' she confessed, 'we were both blamed. I know I ought to have taken him to hospital, but the old doctor did not want it; it was natural that he was not keen that they should know how drunk he was, and there was no way out. The next thing I heard was that he was dead, and that *was* something of a shock. Mr Scott operated (and he is brilliant), but of course a fractured skull is not one of those operations that anyone is mad about.'

'And you got the blame?'

'I and the old doctor, and I believe that the coroner was quite right in what he said. The whole affair was one of the nastiest experiences I have ever had. But Dr Higgs took it worse than I did. He just shut up shop and returned to his home town somewhere near Leeds.'

He listened quietly, then he said, 'You can't go on through the rest of your life being a doctor. There is a bit more to living than that, and you want to get some fun out of life.'

She looked at him with amused eyes, which could dance. She said to him, 'If you think that I intend to waste all those years which I spent in training, you are dead wrong. And I want to be of use to mankind.'

'My goodness! That sounds a bit pious!'

'It isn't pious, it is common sense. I worked hard to learn to do my job well. I stand between my patients and that highly unwelcome guest who always gets through in the end.'

'But you are working a twenty-four-hour day.'

'And a very rewarding one.' She could laugh about it because it meant so much to her. Perhaps he did not understand that she loved her work, and wanted to succeed. 'It is a wonderful feeling when you have pulled a patient through. One drops bricks at times—this always happens in life—and this *was* a brick.' She paused. 'Death plays funny tricks. He is a vile enemy.'

He tried to cheer her.

They stayed outside for their coffee, and the garden now smelt sweetly of June roses, of irises, and of verbena. It was a very beautiful spot. Then, quite suddenly, he became serious, something she had not expected.

'You remember walking on Tennyson Downs?' he said. 'Do you know that was where I found that although I thought I had, I had never been really in love before?'

This startled her. It was something that she had not expected from him. 'Don't let's be silly,' she said, but all the time she knew that deep down inside her there was that stir, the emotion that is love, and whatever happened she must conceal it. He was attractive, of course, that was how he had made his name. In her working life she had never had any great friend, for her spare time had been spent on what she called 'swotting up', so that people did not have time for her. Now she was learning about life itself, and life has a story to tell.

He went on talking. 'I was enraptured when we met that glorious morning on the downs. Do you remember how very soft the turf is there? Like walking on velvet. Both of us were set free from an awful lot of hard work. It was a great experience.'

'I know,' she told him.

'I realize that my life is the very opposite of yours. I deal with emotional dreams—the plays in which I act. You deal with life itself, and that can be hard. But whatever you may say, in life opposites do mix rather well.'

'He mustn't say this,' she told herself. 'This is not the time or the moment, and I must not let the situation run away with me.' Gently she said, 'I did not qualify just to give it up. In a way I am completely dedicated to the job, I think you have to be in order to be able to face it. I am a moderately good surgeon, though my medicine is not so good!'

'You did me proud, and then sending that nice parson chap along. He was jolly decent.'

'He is a very charming man,' she said.

There was something wildly attractive about the garden, with the warm night coming up, and the stars brightening with every moment. Out of the distance there came the song of the nightingale, which she felt was just the final touch. She was sitting in a sweet surround, still and peaceful after the lovely day, with a man whom she liked enormously. She kept telling herself, 'I am not in love with him,' but the fact that she had to insist on this rather gave the idea that she was.

He talked of his new part, not too happily, for the actress playing opposite to him was a girl whom privately he disliked.

'One doesn't act so well with someone whom one dislikes,' he said, 'even if one tries to cover it up.'

'And how do you get out of that in the end?' she asked.

'One acts,' he told her.

They went on to talk of her position here, and how she had become established. It had been very hard going, those first few months. She was grateful that the two good doctors were both very pleasant, and most gracious about her position. Dr Higgs had been horrible, and she thanked heaven that he had gone. It had been impossible to explain the full extent of her difficulties at the inquest (that was a very sore point with her), and this still rankled. She would live it down in time, but for now it worried her.

'I'd forget it,' he said; 'others will.'

'The ridiculous thing is that I have never found it very easy to forget something that has really upset me,' she said.

'Think of me instead,' he suggested with a merry laugh.

They went round the garden picking some flowers for her surgery, before the light completely failed. It was a very happy evening, and as they walked he told her of his own life, which, as he put it, had not been all beer and skittles.

His mother had been most indignant when he first broke the news to her that, like his father, he wanted to go on to the stage. She felt that acting was beneath him, and not a profession at all. Any fool could do it if he tried, was her comment. Then when his younger brother went into the Royal Navy as a cadet, that pacified her somewhat, and she found a certain amount of consolation.

Robin was entirely devoted to the theatre, and although he admitted that there had been periods when he just could not get work, in the end he had always fought through. It had everything to offer, a man could become a star in a single night. He would never have chosen any other career. He told her, 'Chance always comes when you don't expect it. I quivered when the curtain went up for the first time, but within the next four seconds I had found my feet and played like an old hand. I had luck.'

'You did, indeed,' she said. 'I had luck, too, but I get a bit worried now and then. With the two good doctors back in harness, wildly popular men, both of them, and very, very good, I sometimes tend to get my tail well between my legs!'

He smiled at that. 'Either of them an FRCS? Well, there you are! I know it is early days for women in medicine, but they are working their way in, and you had the end of the war as a good start.'

'I know,' and she added, 'I love my work, any job in which you are helping other people is rewarding. *You* teach people to forget the dreariness of their own lives (and most lives are dreary), and that is much the same thing.'

He said he would be down for the weekend fairly often, and he suggested that she should dine there every time he came, but this she could not accept, because of her work. She said she would come if she could. They sat in talking with the dark coming quietly up, and she drove home with the feeling that it had been a wonderful evening, and she had enjoyed it very much indeed.

When he said good night, for a moment his hand lingered on hers, and she drove off knowing that he had the power to carry her right over the top of the world. 'I have got to be careful,' she told herself. In the hall there was a note for her in Miss Willis' handwriting.

'Mrs Sheppard's baby has started. Will you please go round?'

This was a nice thing to find! But it brought her down to earth. She rushed off upstairs and slipped off the pretty dress for a simpler one. She would probably be away all night, for Mrs Sheppard had asked for a special anaesthetic, which meant that the doctor would have to stay with her.

She came down and went straight off to the house. As she approached, she saw the lights burning in the bedroom. 'This,' she said to herself, 'is going to be a long session, for she wants Twilight Sleep, and that means a long job.'

When she went upstairs, she found a capable nurse with her, and she immediately got down to work. Now she had forgotten the converted forge, and the lovely dinner. She had forgotten everything except the fact that a new life was coming into the world, and she must do all in her power to get it here without the patient being in too much pain, or too anxious.

'I can trust you, Doctor,' she said.

'I promise you I'll do all I can, and I shan't leave you.'

Anna told herself that she would feel something like a two-day-old poached egg tomorrow, but this was part of the job. It was nine in the morning when the baby came into the world, a lovely little girl. Anna would be back on duty at ten, as she should be, and none of her patients must know how tired she was.

The nurse was good at her job, and the moment Anna had examined the child and found it perfect, she could go, and she got home in time for surgery.

'It is a strange life,' she thought, with the quiet dinner last night, sitting in the garden, and Robin verging on the love story which somehow she did not want to take place. Her life was now absorbed by this place. He would call it living in a rut, but this is what happens to doctors.

She was sure that a way would be shown her, remembering that this was always what her mother used to say, and perhaps with truth. When you are in the dark of this world, a way is always shown you. She had the feeling that for the moment she had lost her way.

CHAPTER EIGHT

Anna could not dine with Robin the next Saturday, for last thing in the afternoon there had to be a critical operation on someone who had been injured in an accident. When she managed to get to the operation Dr Graves was there. She telephoned Robin, but he was irritated, and said surely she could do something about it? He did not understand that doctors can't 'do something about it', for their work is to get on with the job. In medical life it is necessary to put the troubles of others before one's own pleasure, and she performed the operation and found that somehow it tired her far more than she had anticipated.

There was a great deal of work to settle and it was difficult to get things sorted out. Always it seemed that her private life suffered for it. Was this the one job in the world in which one had no private life? It seemed at times to be very much like it. She had felt that when the two doctors returned from the front, life would be easier, though perhaps not so profitable. In fact, it was not. And now young Dr Webb had died and Dr Higgs had retired.

She felt thankful that her background was

changing, for the transition from war to peace was already making a great difference to England. Things were beginning to settle down, and she was grateful.

The operation was extremely difficult, and afterwards Matron had coffee ready for the two surgeons in her own room, where they could talk. It seemed that they had come closer together in the theatre. She thought he was worried, not about the patient, for the operation went without a flaw, but he had heard from his wife in the States. She had, as Anna knew, remarried, and about two years ago she had had an operation which she wrote about as being 'nothing much, only a small lump in the breast'. By the extent of the operation he had presumed that it was malignant and she did not like to admit it. He had heard from her again, and now strongly suspected that she had a secondary growth.

'A secondary?'

'It seems like it.'

She knew that he would never have told her if he had not become extremely worried about it.

'It is additionally difficult as her second marriage has crashed. He cleared off and now she wants to return to Weston, she says to die.' He spoke quite calmly, sipping from the cup of coffee as he did so. Then he added: 'She could be right about that, of course, but I don't know what to do. I . . . I never expected this.'

Very quietly Anna asked him, 'How do you really feel about it?'

He was one of those men who always speak the truth, and he declared that to deceive a patient was quite wrong. People face up to crises far better if they have faith in their doctor, believe that he knows the best thing to do for them, and will do it. He said that he knew his ex-wife was in a bad way, but the old adage, 'While there is life, there is hope,' was true. She very much admired his attitude to his work, and his complete devotion to it.

They talked it over, and Anna knew that his wife's behaviour had gone a long way towards killing his love for her, but he still felt in some small way responsible. When she left, he came to the door with her to see her off.

They parted, and for some reason there were tears in her eyes. She knew that he was deeply sympathetic to his wife, but he could hardly offer a home in the small town where all the scandal had started, and where everybody talked. It was doubtful if her life could be prolonged for any length of time if she had a secondary growth, and Anna did not know what to advise.

She went over to the Old Forge at Burbage to dine with Robin again. Afterwards they took their coffee into the garden as before, with the strong smell of pinks in flower (they always reminded her of a tube of toothpaste which had stood by her father's basin!). Robin was working too hard, and although he said that he had quite recovered from the crash, she was not too sure, and he was a difficult man to influence, because he always wanted his own way.

'Why don't you ask for a couple more days down here?' she said.

'Because there isn't a chance. This filming has taken longer than anyone expected, and I have also got a first night just ahead of me.'

'Yes, of course, but it is a strain for you.'

'I'm pretty strong, and I feel OK now. You leave my job to me, and I shall be quite all right.' Then he pointedly changed the subject. 'I don't think you earn sufficient money down here, you ought to charge more for your services, don't you think so?'

'For one thing, I am a new girl here. I have to take things quietly until I am firmly settled in. I admit I *am* settling in fine, life has been good to me, and the two doctors who came back have been a very great help to me. I believe this is going to be the luckiest year of my whole life, but I can't afford to play tricks.'

He nodded assent. 'You've done well. I know that doctors prosper on other people's misfortunes, of which every one of us has many, but this is the way life goes on.'

The stars were coming out once more, tiny silver twinkles here and there in the night sky. She said, 'As long as we can help our patients, we are happy, and so are they. I am loving my career, and would not change it for any other in the world.'

He talked again of his family and his early life. He said he had an elder brother who was a solicitor, but that was not his own line of country, and they never got him into it. He said, 'When it came to my turn, I said no, I wanted to act. You should have seen the fit my mother threw!'

'I can imagine it.'

He could laugh about it now, but, as all the world knows, an actor's life can be very much on the here-today-and-gone-tomorrow principle. He had been so lucky. 'There is a lot to be said for the black cat, the horseshoe, the white heather, and the sun coming out at the right moment,' and he smiled at the thought.

At the same time, he freely admitted that

he did get fits of nerves. Had she got an antidote for that? She said she could supply what she called a first-class pick-me-up, but that was all, or some bromide, which was a calm-me-down. She said she believed that every good actor suffered from nerves, and found them very distressing.

She went home. Somehow she was tired, and she felt that she should get back, though she didn't want to go. He was such a very good companion, and he had undoubtedly made her find her girlhood all over again; it had been plunged into a sea of training and exams, and fighting for the lives of others. She had adored that weekend at Ventnor, and she hoped he would never go out of her life.

When she got home there was a message from Lady Porth. Would she ring up in the morning?

'Now what has *she* been up to?' Anna asked herself.

CHAPTER NINE

She rang Lady Porth in the morning, and she asked if Anna could come and see her. Of course, she said, and gave her a time. It was a smaller surgery than usual, nothing serious, and they came and went fairly easily. Apparently yesterday the son and heir had not been well, just sick, nothing very much. They thought that he had eaten something that he had not told them about, and this was what had happened as a result.

He had been better this morning, but just before Anna arrived, he was sick again. She went upstairs to the beautiful night nursery, in which she felt that her own future had been built! Nanny was sitting with the child, holding his hand.

'Oh dear, this *is* nasty,' she said. It was quite obvious that he had eaten something he should not have done, though how he had got it, nobody could think. Nanny had asked him, and he knew nothing, then Anna had a talk without Nanny being there. In the end it transpired that he had been playing in the garden when an old gipsy had come up the drive selling sweets in a big basket. He had his pocket money, and spent it on some, then decided that if he took them indoors, Nanny would probably take them from him, so he had eaten the lot!

He felt ill soon after.

'You know that was a very silly thing to do,' she told him, but kindly. 'Those sweets gipsies sell are very badly made, in dirty conditions, and then they make you ill.'

She went over him with the greatest care, deciding that this was merely a passing worry which was getting better under its own steam; being the only son, he had a family who got agonized if anything went wrong. He was, of course, a spoilt son, and a bit of a cry-baby at that, for he had found that if he cried for his own way, he probably got it.

One has to understand the patient, and Anna thought that she did understand Eddie. It was a pity that they had not a second son, for they staked everything on Eddie, which was not very good for him.

She went downstairs and was offered a sherry. Lady Porth wanted to talk. Anna might have had a fairly easy morning, but often days become busier as they go along, and she did not particularly want a talk at this moment, but she sat down in the library.

Lady Porth was much happier when she

heard Anna's diagnosis. She said, 'I know we should not spoil him so much, but he is the only heir in the whole family. Everyone else has daughters. It makes one feel a wee bit unsafe, but I . . . I did want to ask you . . . I have not felt at all well lately, and I wondered if I might be enceinte?'

They went into the details. Anna prayed that this was the case, for it would make things so much better for the heir, who could not help knowing he was of immense value to the family.

Anna thought that she was several months pregnant, but she was a delicate woman prone to ill health on the smallest excuse, and she desperately wanted another child. 'I don't like having only Eddie,' she said. 'I want another son, and I should like to be sure that it *is* another son. Surely something can be done to influence the sex?'

'I'm afraid there is nothing at all. I know the Russians always say that the little Tsarevitch, the Tsar's fifth child, came through a special diet, but I very much doubt that. The sex is determined at the moment of conception and is a pure matter of chance. But given time you can easily have another son.'

'I think,' said Lady Porth, 'that at the present stage in the history of the world, we ought to be able to make sure.'

'It might rather spoil things if we could,' and Anna smiled as she said it.

When she got home she found a message from Robin Grant. He was just off back to London, and this was to say *au revoir*. But he would be down again soon, and he would send her a ticket for the show.

She was very sorry he had gone.

She turned back to her practice, as any good doctor does. She had some things that she wanted to change, and this would take time. She really had been intensely fortunate since she came to Weston, and although she had been worried, wondering if she would ever get enough patients to enable her to build up a good practice, she now realized that she was settling in and need no longer be apprehensive. She liked the change that peace was making to the place, the contact with new people, and all the hope in the world for a new life with greater opportunities.

She had settled into the life here, after the difficulties of her start during the end of the war, then meeting the two well-loved doctors returned from the front, happy to find that they did not resent her, but accepted her. The practice was changing, of course, but it would not be such hard work as it had been in the beginning. She soon heard more about Dr Richard Graves.

He had won the MC for going over the top to recover a wounded man who lay screaming in no man's land, hoping to save his life. The man had died, but the deed had been done. Dr Graves had been particularly brave, and he had received a nasty wound. One day when they had been doing an operation together, he did say, 'It was pretty awful. Thank God there will never be another war, for this one has caused too much suffering; we could never face that agony again.'

'They do say that this will be the last of all wars,' she replied, and devoutly hoped this would turn out to be true.

'Yes, that's what people say.' He paused a moment, then he said, 'But primitive instinct lingers. People always say they will never fight again because war isn't worth it, and then the whole thing starts off from the beginning once more.'

'I'm afraid you could be right there.'

She would never know why he started again to talk about his wife. He was deeply anxious for her, apparently her condition was even worse than he had anticipated. She was ill in Los Angeles. She had always been a rather restless woman who travelled round the world and could never settle down. Now she wanted to come back to English doctors, because she disliked the men who were looking after her out there. She was homesick, very wretched, and he did not know what to do about her.

As he lit a cigaratte he said, 'I wonder if I ought to get her back here, where she could die in peace. It would be a ghastly journey for her, and today this is such an entirely different world. I just don't know what to do.'

'Do you suppose she could stand the journey? If she had a rough passage, it would be absolutely terrible for her. She could even die during it.'

'I agree,' he said, as though he felt there was no argument, but in his heart he was desperately worried.

She realized that he was lost in an abyss of uncertainty and wanted advice, yet was not prepared to take it. He admitted that he had even thought of taking time off to go and fetch her himself. She listened quietly.

'I wonder if that would be wise.'

'I am quite distraught, for I really don't know what to do.' Then the telephone rang, and it was a message from his home. A friend who was ill wanted to see him. He came back to tell her. It was a very old friend indeed, and because of this he did not like to hold back. Then he got into his coat, and said half-laughingly, 'Before you came here, the town was having a rather bad time with those two old boys with whom you nearly became the third partner. You may not have thought it was for the best, but you were well out of it.'

Then he went off to see his patient.

* * *

She felt that she had lived through several years since she had arrived here, with the war ending so soon after she was settled in, and then getting down to her practice to fight every inch of the way. The world around her had suddenly come into a new phase of living. Crazed young men discharged from the forces, and buying motor-bikes as fast as they could; the eternal accidents on those motor-bikes; it seemed that the roads of England were even more perilous than the trenches of France. The dancing era had broken into the gay young world. Everybody danced. It was the age of relaxation from war, and enjoying the happiness of living. A time when new houses began to spring up everywhere, when people could buy things denied them for so many years; she would never forget her perfect ecstasy the first time she could buy a real iced cake.

The world changed entirely. It took on a new speed of living, and people had grown more daring. The horrors of war had sobered everyone down at the time, but now it became exactly the opposite; it was gay, it was amusing, it was a new mode of life which somehow nobody had thought to be possible.

Anna found herself divided two ways. Half of her was the girl who wanted to dance and enjoy herself, for one is young only the once; the other half wanted to build up a steady practice, which was very hard work, and which, she confessed, at times tired her out.

'I have got to be a doctor *first*,' she kept telling herself, 'because the whole of my future depends on this, and I have got to work hard even if the other two have come back.'

A week or so later, the housekeeper who kept Dr Graves's home rang her up. She seemed to be considerably worried.

'I wanted to know if you could come over, Doctor,' she said. 'The doctor .. he has had a bad turn, and I need help badly.'

'I'll come over immediately.'

She did not even take a coat, but went out and across the street, to the rather modern

1907 house on the far side of the road. The housekeeper was at the door, and opened it before Anna actually got there.

'There's been a telegram, Doctor,' she said. 'Mrs Graves died in hospital this morning. He . . . he is ever so upset.'

She said, 'Yes, yes, of course. Where do I find him?'

He was in the surgery. Like most other country surgeries, she supposed, a place without personality, nothing to disclose the sort of man that he was, his interests, or his happinesses and unhappinesses. It showed his profession, his care for others, but nothing about himself. He was sitting at the desk, as she presumed he always did when he saw people. She went in, and across towards him.

She said, 'I've come to see if there is anything that I can do to help you.'

He turned and looked at her, and his face had gone quite grey with worry, the colour that she hated seeing creep over anyone.

'I've had bad news.'

'Yes, I know.' She saw he had a half-drunk glass of whisky beside him. 'I'd have some more of that,' she suggested, knowing that he was a most abstemious man. 'It would help you.'

Almost automatically he took up the glass

and drank it down, without a single word of protest. The fact that he said nothing made her realize that he was not himself, for he was not the man to accept orders, though she believed that in his present mood he would do everything she said.

Probably this was the best thing that could have happened, for Anna knew that his wife had wanted to come home, which would have been impossible for her in her present condition. She herself knew that this was the best way out of a situation which could only have become more and more difficult.

If his wife had lived, she might have made a desperate attempt to return, and Anna felt that fate had saved the poor thing a great deal of pain and trouble. Her return would only have added to the general complications. Now the doctor sat there quietly, a dark man, his face ashen in contrast to his very black hair, and his very blue eyes.

He said, 'I feared she would attempt the journey, and die at sea. That was a frightful thought.'

'I know,' and she spoke gently. 'It is, of course, the best thing, though the hardest to bear, and she might so easily have died on the journey over.'

'She might indeed.' Then he spoke very

quietly, as though he were trying to convince himself that life always acts for the best. 'She could have lived a few months more, but one would not have wanted that for her. I . . . I'm glad it is all over now, but at the same time it is a shock. It has to be."

In the end he said, 'Life has done the very best thing, of course, but when one is the person affected, it is hard to bear.'

'I know. It is a dreadful thing to be glad when someone is relieved of great suffering, and she must have had a very bad time.'

He said, 'Thank you. You are very comforting when I am feeling down.'

There was so little that she could do. She suggested a sleeping draught tonight, and said that she would take over his duties for him, so that he could have calls transferred to her. But he did not want her to do this. In the end she forced to him to agree. He would go to bed immediately, as she asked, and she prescribed a draught for him.

That was when Miss Willis rang her. There was a message from Lord Porth; Lady Porth was not very well. She had been very sick, a bad start to the night. Anna said that she would run out to them now.

'I shall have to go,' she said.

'It was very good of you to come.'

'Promise me you'll take the sleeping draught? No slipping it down the sink!'

'No slipping it down the sink,' he said quite gravely, 'and that is a promise.' And then as she went to the door, 'I . . . I am very grateful to you. You have been much more help than you know.'

She went home, got the car out, and went straight off to the Porths. As she turned the corner by the church, it struck eleven. 'This,' she told herself, 'is one of those nights that will never end.' She realized that Lady Porth was a patient who got worked up. She was a woman who was constantly depressed, and harboured what she called forebodings. She was a nervous woman, and scared for her health.

Anna went straight up to Lady Porth's bedroom, with the soft azure hangings against pale woodwork, which gave a very pretty effect. Instantly Anna knew that it was the same old story. She had eaten something which had started off one of these rather formidable attacks. In the old days it would have been attributed to a bilious attack. She was a very careless eater, of course.

Anna stayed with her until after one o'clock, doing what she could to help, and when she finally left, Lady Porth was almost out of pain, and probably would sleep.

Last thing she had a word with Lord Porth, who was most distressed. He was afraid that if these attacks went on they might affect his wife's future. Anna said, 'I am going to put her on a strict diet. I want her first to go right away and have a good holiday, as soon as she can. It may be an affliction she eventually gets over. Let's wait and see how things are. We don't want this sort of thing always happening.'

She got home, and went to bed to snatch what rest she could get. 'It's a hard life,' she told herself. She was really sorry about the last two cases she had had, and there was so little she could do about either of them. She did not know what was causing Lady Porth's trouble.

Next morning she got a letter from Robin Grant.

He was not at all happy about the rehearsals of the new play, and was worried about its future. I did not 'run' well, he felt, but he enclosed a ticket for her for the first night. Nobody liked the producer very much, which is always a bad beginning for any play. All through his letter to her he managed to infuse her with his personal uneasiness. He looked forward to seeing her on the opening night, and it would be a break for her. She had to admit that continual medical work (and it asked day and night of her) was tedious, and she did feel the stress of it. It was so strange that in her training days she had always thought that a country practice would be a very comfortable method of existence, and now she was learning how wrong she had been.

It seemed that some occult power took a delight in having patients urgently needing attention at the same time, in opposite directions.

Again she was sent for by Lord Porth. Lady Porth was much better, but he was anxious that nothing was being done to avert the return of these bad attacks. He very much wanted another child and was glad that she was again pregnant. But his wife was subject to these attacks of nerves, and it was very difficult to soothe her down. Unless she could control these times when she got so agitated, she might risk a miscarriage. It transpired that she had done this twice already. No wonder they were anxious.

Anna tried to persuade her to have a quiet holiday and not do too much, for there was the coming of the new baby to be considered, the one both she and her husband wanted so desperately badly. There was no reason for them to worry. But at all costs she must not worry.

'Let her get over this attack, then take her away for a short while. We want her to get out of the habit of having these attacks, because I think it has become a habit, and once started they are difficult to stop.'

She could not stay long, for a call came through for her; there had been yet another road accident, and a patient was waiting for her at the hospital. She was unhappy because these folks were so worried about Lady Porth's attacks, but she dared not delay, and she had to get back to her work, for other people needed her attention.

She had a very busy day, and that night she received another letter from Robin Grant. He was getting more and more disturbed about the new play, and he really did not think it was good enough. It was, he said, so easy to get a bad press, and that would finish it. He had booked a room for her for the first night, and privately she was looking forward to it enormously, anything for a change, for after a time a doctor's work does get boring, and tiring. In hospital one had some exciting cases, but here one got the routine of children with the 'tummy ache', women being difficult, men who wanted an excuse for not going to work, accidents at outlying farms, and all the rest of it. It seemed that one was always behind time, for the distances were great. She tore off to some remote village to see a child with pains, dreaming of an appendix, only to find it was nothing at all. One had too many of these cases.

Next afternoon, because she had been to an outlying farm in the neighbourhood, she dropped in to see Hugh Felton. The rectory was untidy as usual, a house which never got a proper turn-out, as she could see, but he was a sympathetic and comforting man, and at this particular moment in her life this was just what she needed most.

He said, 'You're worried, aren't you?' and she admitted that this was true. She had too much to do, and too little time in which to do it. Dr Jackson, with his funny old bike, had suddenly retired, not that he had ever been of much help, but he had been another pair of hands. Since she had arrived here, the medical conditions of the place had altered considerably.

He said, 'Life does this for all of us. It changes all the time, and there is nothing we can do about it. It seems to me that the coming of peace has changed us more than did the war itself. It *is* a new world, and I think we shall need some time in which to get used to it.'

'Yes, I know,' she confessed. 'But how awful it would have been if we had lost, and I rather thought we might at the time when Lord Kitchener died.'

'We lost far too much anyway,' and he said it quietly. She knew that he was thinking of those miles of graves in France, thousands of them, the very flower of young England, and all *so* young, who should have had their lives before them. It appalled one to think of it.

'We can never make that good again,' she said.

He spoke firmly. 'You must not think that. Things happen, and there seems to be a certain sequence in our lives. Realize this, for it is important to our living. I am sure that these things happen for a purpose, and the older I get the more convinced I am. When you came to see me and operated on my leg and got me right again, that was with a purpose. I . . . I can never be grateful enough.'

'It is really and truly getting better now? No more pain?' she asked.

'Little spasms now and then, but getting better all the time.'

He was such a charming man, and very

reliable. He asked after Robin Grant, and was concerned that he was worried about the new play that was coming on.

'He is very much tied up with it at the moment. But that is so with all jobs. He is not at all happy about it. And that makes me unhappy for him.'

Hugh Felton understood, but he said, 'Never be upset about people worrying. The big troubles in life flash round the corner on to us, and those are the crises that really matter. One does not recognize their enormity until they are actually here. I have seen this happen so many times. I suppose every actor gets worried to death about a new play. It means everything to him.'

It was very pleasant and comfortable to be sitting here having tea in the rather untidy room, which she had grown to like. About the place there was the air of home, of kindness and of generosity. Before she left she warned him not to overdo his work. He had still got to take life quietly with that leg of his and rest it as much as he could.

'Surely a little weeding would be all right now?'

'Well, I should hardly recommend it, but I doubt if patience will be your cup of tea!' She wished that she could come to visit him more frequently, but her practice was increasing, which meant that she had more visits to pay, and her surgeries took longer.

That night Dr Graves came in to sup with her. It was a very quiet supper, beautifully cooked; she owed a lot to Miss Willis, who never minded how hard she worked. Anna rather hoped that the doctor would tell her some details about his wife, but he did not talk about her very much. He had heard from the States that she had had a sudden heart attack. There had been a post mortem and they had found that there was a growth in the breast. It had certainly been the kind way out, if death can be kind; and there were moments when Anna felt that it was the solution, though she hated admitting it, but no one could want a person to live on in suffering.

He changed the subject, and told her that he had become a doctor because his father and elder brother were both doctors, and he had to earn his living.

'I just drifted into it. Not particularly attracted by it, but it seemed to be the thing to do. Then I did get interested, surgery absorbed me. That is the miracle worker. My brother is in Harley Street, but I don't think he does very well there, it is one of those things, but he has the right address, which I suppose is something. I should hate that. You never see the end of the case; patients visit you, and go away, you never know how it has worked out, and I like to know.'

'I do, too,' she said.

They sat on talking for a long time, and it was a slack night when neither of them was called out. She felt that it had helped him to have someone with whom to have a talk. She liked him. He had both feet on the ground, had known trouble, and although he was going through a bad time now, he would overcome it and start all over again. When he left she knew that he was happier, just because he had had someone to talk to.

'I am thankful for that,' she told herself.

CHAPTER TEN

Anna went up to London on the morning of the day when Robin Grant's new play was coming on. She had the night off, and she was going to enjoy every moment of it. The idea was that they would sup together after the play, for it would be quite impossible for them to go out beforehand.

She was finding that actors and actresses were the most superstitious people, and knew that he was worried to death about the whole thing. He felt that the play was under-rehearsed, and that it was being born under some unlucky star. She went round to his dressing-room before the play started, and did her best to cheer him up, but this was difficult.

'Do try to remember that half the things we expect to go wrong, go right,' she said.

But he was not happy about it, and she realized that the only thing was to get the horror of the first night over, and then perhaps he would relax and feel better. She went back to the front of the House, and the place was packed. The playwright was very famous; as she told herself, it was unlikely that he would write a bad play, but of course one really never knew. Poor plays have been written by even the most illustrious.

The orchestra had begun when she slipped into her seat; then it softly died down, and the great curtain swept up. She knew that she was desperately apprehensive, and it was something so entirely out of her world that she might be over-timid about it.

The play was not a success. Robin had predicted this; everyone had worked frightfully hard, but...

She liked the start, it was original, and when Robin came on he got a tremendous reception. The cast were doing their utmost, but the truth is that even the most magnificent cast cannot pull a bad play together, and she was well aware of its faults. The suspense was not sustained. She shuddered when she thought of tomorrow's reviews, by which the play would possibly live or die.

She knew that at first Robin was wildly nervous, but he certainly put into the part everything that he had got, though it was not sufficient. He must have been pleased with his reception, but, as he had said to her beforehand, 'It is the play itself that is tonight's bogy.'

She went behind the scenes as he had asked

her to do, and into a world which she felt would always be strange to her. She found the contrast of the stone alleyways (none too clean) so different from the luxuries of some of the dressing-rooms, where everything was done to put the actors and actresses at their ease. In his dressing-room it was cosy, there were a lot of people all trying to convince him that it had been very successful, but he knew too much about it. They went out to dine together, sick of the crowds and wanting to get out of the theatre. He had chosen a quiet little restaurant where one could eat very late indeed, and in peace. He wanted peace after the effort of the night.

'For now, let's just rest and eat,' she suggested, 'and I am speaking as a doctor. After that strain, and with no supper inside you, you need something to build you up, and a drink.'

The food was good, and the restaurant prettily lit by flickering candlelight, the tall red candles standing in glass containers on pale blue cloths, and with bowls of flowers beneath each light. After a time he felt better.

He said, 'First nights are the most awful strain, however well the play goes, and this was *not* a good enough play to travel very far. I knew it was a dud when we started to rehearse, and although we did make a lot of alterations, they were insufficient to pull it round. I bet the critics kill it for us!'

'Don't look ahead,' she told him. 'Tomorrow never comes.'

'Oh, doesn't it just!' said he, 'that is a very old-fashioned idea; if it wasn't for tomorrow being round the next corner, we could have a far jollier time today.'

She was sorry for him, for he was truly worried about the play, and she wanted to comfort him, but did not know how to do so. So they talked of themselves. Of the island, and the peace that always seemed to lie over it, like a pretty coverlet; their first walk when they had met on Tennyson Downs, dancing together that night at the hotel. It had been a spontaneous, happy meeting.

He drove her back to the hotel, and they planned to lunch next day. When she saw the comments in the newspapers, she felt truly sorry for him, for he had put a tremendous lot of work into the play, and the reviewers had been extremely plain-spoken. She blamed them, but remembered that this was their job, and she had to admit that the play was not up to standard.

They had a rather hurried lunch, for she was catching a fairly early train home, and he was most depressed. But every review had praised *his* work with an extremely ill-written part. Not for the world would she have asked him how he really felt about it, and he glossed over it all. Then he said that probably it would not run for very long (she had thought this herself).

'There is no actor in the world who has not had a bit of bother with a bad play at some time or another. I should not have accepted the part, but it was a lead, and I wanted it.' He said it with regret.

It seemed to be the most difficult career. One had to accept a part to keep oneself before the public, and then, if it was a poor one, one was blamed for being a fool ever to have taken it on.

'But that's life,' he said, and then, over black coffee, 'Let's talk about you. You don't have to act in life, you fight death.'

'I know,' she said, ' and it is a bit of a blow that in some cases the patient has to die. I don't think I shall ever get used to that.'

'You were in luck when you had the Porth heir to treat. He won't die for a long time. I wish they had another son.'

She was not sure if this was not a try-out to test her as to what she would disclose. She said, 'Yes, that would be very nice for them,' rather vaguely, and left it at that. Long, long ago, when she had first begun her career, she learned that silence is a doctor's star turn.

He was too much worried about last night's play to keep away from it for very long, and he admitted that he had a second play up his sleeve. He thought he was going to accept the leading part after this morning's papers, because undoubtedly last night's show was already on the way out.

She knew that he was as anxious as anyone was, and she wished that she could reassure him that the play would last, but it certainly had not maintained interest. When she had read the reviews she had recognized that it was the flop she had thought whilst she was watching it, and her big anxiety was lest the flop should have an effect on the actors' careers.

She went back to the country with the knowledge that the play would probably not last a fortnight. Robin did not see her off at the station, for he was far too deeply involved in his commitments. He did telephone her later, at home, admitting that he had expected the bad notices; but a failure is something that every actor has at least once in his life, and if you happen to be born unlucky it recurs at other times. But whatever happened, everybody got it one day or another.

As she travelled home she sat listening to the steady throb of the wheels, and she wondered how it was that play-readers do not spot the errors before a play ever gets on to the stage. The cost of producing a show is so high that to have a failure is a disaster which it is hard to stand up against.

When she got back there was a pile of messages, and she had to make five visits when it was already the late afternoon. Richard Graves had been acting as locum for her and had been surprised by the number of calls, but there was nothing really urgent, except for Lady Porth, who had rung up.

'I'll ring her back,' Anna said, for the note attached to this message had marked it urgent. She did ring back. It was not as urgent as all that, but could she go round first thing in the morning?

'Of course,' she agreed.

It was one of those high summer evenings, when the country is so utterly lovely, and somehow she could not think how she had ever gone to London when this part of the world was looking so radiant with the sweet of the year.

She turned in through the open park gates,

with the green spreading before her, and the great trees on either side, an avenue of silent sentinels, and every little while a flashing view of the house itself between the big branches.

She hoped that the coming baby was not going to be troublesome. Lady Porth was one of those women who can be very easily upset, for she happened to take things deeply to heart, and could not cure herself of this failing. She fainted for the slightest reason, and got worked up over nothing. Of course everyone is different in personality, and this is something that a doctor has to cope with. Now privately Anna was anxious lest the patient miscarried, she was the sort of woman who would do this, and had done it before. The butler opened the door almost immediately to her, and said that her Ladyship wanted her to go straight upstairs to her. She was not herself this morning.

'I fear the worst,' Anna told herself.

She went up the magnificent staircase, which curled its way up, and along the landing to the big bedroom at the far end. Lady Porth was still in bed, looking very pale. She had had a bad fainting attack that morning, and had fallen and hurt herself; she also was terrified lest this should bring on a miscarriage.

'Now don't think of silly things like that,' Anna told her. She did her best to calm her down. She must rest and take life very easily for a few days. There was, for the moment, no need to worry, but she simply must take care. She knew that she was giving the patient confidence, by talking to her like this, and she prescribed some medicine. When she had quietened her down and made sure that, provided the lady did what she was told, everything would be all right, she went downstairs to where Lord Porth was waiting for her in the comfortable library.

'Is she all right?' he asked. 'I am very anxious for her.'

'There is no need to be. She is going to be all right, but she will have to take care. You must try not to let it upset her, for she is one of those people who get very easily worked up.'

'Yes, I know she is.'

The butler brought in some coffee and some very nice biscuits; the Porths always did one well, as she told herself, and she was grateful for this, because she had had her breakfast interrupted in the middle, for a child had been brought in with a broken nose.

Anna said, 'She ought to have quite a quiet week, resting all the time. It has been very hot weather, of course, and this is no help to her. Don't encourage her to make an invalid of herself, she needs a spot of cheering up, something to give her confidence. You must not encourage her to think that it will go wrong, for there is absolutely no reason why it should.'

He nodded. 'I have faith in you, had from the very first, after the awful old chaps we were left with in this place. The war cleared the country of good doctors, and that was *not* funny. You will see after her, won't you?'

'Of course.'

On her way back, she called in at the rectory to see how Hugh Felton was getting on, and if he had kept his word to stop fiddling about in the garden too much, when he ought to be resting the leg. He was well and radiant, and enchanted to see her. The garden looked quite wonderful, and they went round it together. He gave her a big bunch of roses and some vegetables to take home with her.

She said, 'Thank you. But do remember that you can't play tricks with difficult legs, it is not worth trying. If you were a child, it would have recovered more quickly.'

'The pain has gone,' he told her, 'and I want to try to use it.'

'I know, but give it care, for this *is* important. It will need care for some time yet, whether you like it or not, and then it will last you out for the rest of your life. I promise you that.'

He grumbled that if he had known this when he had the operation done, he would probably have demurred, but in the end he admitted that she had done a grand job, and that he owed her a lot. His worry was that he could not pay as much as he should, for his stipend would not allow for that, and he said it pathetically.

She replied, 'That is not your fault. I myself have been hard-up enough in my life to know what it means. And when I arrived here I had spent almost my last farthing on buying the house and furniture, only to find that the old chaps didn't really want me as a partner.'

'Because they had got that ghastly nephew cheaper!' and he laughed.

'I should not have put it in those words.'

It was delightful being with him. Like being at home. They could talk of the people and he was very helpful at giving her advice about the difficulties she might meet with them. Like old Mrs Barker, who would not have a doctor because she adhered to Christian Science and believed that medicine was wrong.

'It is hard to get round that,' she said. 'She

devoutly believes in her religion.'

'Is she really very ill?'

'I don't know. She might be. One would have to make tests to be sure, and she will not see any doctor.'

'How did she come to tell you?'

'It was at a garden fête, when we were all wandering round the lawn buying all sorts of things, and then she told me. I can't think what came over her. Save that deep down inside her she probably felt that she had to tell someone.'

'Could she be in danger?'

'I really don't know. One is always apprehensive, and I should love to help her.'

He said, 'I don't know her very well or I would have a word with her, and try myself to persuade her.'

She shook her head. 'We can't do that, I'm afraid. She has a perfect right not to have a doctor if she feels that way, and her religion is against her having one.'

He said, 'We ought to do something.'

She said quietly, 'In life there are so many times when we ought to do something, but this is not one of them.'

'She has her Christian Science,' he said, 'and they all seem to get immense comfort out of it, but at the same time I feel that we ought to help her.'

'How can we?' she said rather helplessly.

How lovely it was out here in the garden, with the bees making their soporific murmuring, and the heat haze lying over it all! She felt at peace with the world. She knew that he was really better, and eager to get back to his work in the garden.

Then he changed the subject.

He said, 'I am so glad that you had a good time in London, though sorry that the play was a failure. Awful for the actors and actresses, though of course that must be the risk that all of them are prepared to take. But after weeks of rehearsal and preparation, to have the show off within a week or two is the end.'

'Yes, it certainly must be,' she said.

Then she had to return to her rounds, the boot of her car full of vegetables and flowers. She had a heavy list of visits, and she knew she had already spent too long with Hugh Felton, but it was one of those mornings when somehow she had felt that she must have a little relaxation. Hugh was a very helpful person, and always solicitous, just the right type for a village parson.

That evening Lady Porth rang her up to say that she was feeling considerably better, and Anna thanked heaven for that. She was a woman who lived on her imagination, the most difficult patient to see through this sort of thing.

As she took her evening surgery she thought that undoubtedly she would never go back to London to work. After the kindly friendliness of a country practice, the getting to know nice people, and being not only the doctor but the visitor so welcome everywhere, she could not return to London, as she had originally thought she might do.

Today it had been lovely doing her rounds through a glorious countryside that was glowing with summer. The ditches wore a bridal veil, with cow parsely standing high in a white lace of its own, and the wild roses were everywhere. There was about the countryside that rare beauty which one does not see in London. There, one hardly knows that spring has come, or summer is here, though perhaps one sees when the tarnishing fingers of autumn touch the leaves. Anna knew that she loved the country for its personality.

She was called out later to a house standing well out of the town , where one of the servants was suspected to have scarlet fever, and the whole household had panicked over it. They were quite wrong. Whilst she was there, trying to convince the lady of the house that it was a very ordinary rash and nothing to be afraid of, the village policeman came to the house for her. He had been phoned to get hold of her, for there had been a motor accident on the far side of Drayland, and a doctor was badly wanted. She went off to it at once.

She found the spot because a broken-down tradesman's cart was standing on the verge, and there was someone lying on the grass. One of the two policemen on the spot was worried for her. 'It 'ent a job for a lady, miss,' was what he said.

'I'm a doctor and quite used to nasty things. I have come here to help the patient if I can,' and she went to where the man lay.

She looked at him, and mercifully he was unconscious. He was bleeding badly, and her first effort was to attempt to stop this. She worked calmly and with determination, the two policemen watching her. The patient had a broken arm, and a leg twisted under him, for he had been flung out of the car he was driving, and by the look of things the gear lever had got in the way.

'This is a hospital case,' she said, 'can you get an ambulance to take him into the town?'

The police had done their job well, for they had already sent for the ambulance, and were expecting it to arrive at any moment. The man looked dreadfully ill, and she gave him an injection, to make sure that he did not come to before the ambulance got him to hospital. The police knew he was a well-born man, coming from one of the big houses in the neighbourhood, and the son of a gentleman ('A real gentleman' was the way they put it). He had been expelled from school when he was in his teens, and had been more or less in trouble ever since. The policemen thought that he had tried to commit suicide, for he had done this once before, and each time he had bungled it and had missed the mark.

His wife had left him ('Ever such a lady,' the senior policeman told her), and that had been perhaps the final straw which had determined him not to mend his ways and settle down to sound and sensible living, but to end it all.

Anna knew that there was very little more that she could do for him. She feared that he would be permanently lamed by the accident, for the leg was badly crushed. There would be very little that one could say to him to try to encourage him not to attempt to commit suicide again (not that she would admit that he *had* tried to do this; to her it was an ordinary everyday road accident).

She waited for the ambulance to come, then followed it to the hospital. There she operated as soon as they had got him prepared for it. He did not come round. He died before the evening, and in a way she was thankful for his own sake, for it seemed that he had nothing left to live for. It was cases like this which made her desperately sorry for humanity in general. This young man—for he still was a young man—had been born able to live on only the one way, and it could never have got him very far. But no doctor likes losing a young patient who should have an enjoyable existence lying ahead of him, a happy home, a kind wife, and children to bless him.

She went back to have a very late lunch. Miss Willis had been getting quite distracted with anxiety as to what had happened to her, and she felt very sad about it all.

She went down the little main street where the shops were doing brisk business, the housewives still shopping, and chattering together. As she turned into her own garden she saw to her amazement that two men were taking down the 'For Sale' notice board on the old doctors' house. The board offering it for sale had been up only for a couple of weeks, and they were asking a fairly high price, but there was a very ready sale for houses just now.

'I do hope that someone nice is coming there,' she said to herself as she turned into her own house, very late already.

Of course Miss Willis knew all about it! There was little of that nature that Miss Willis did not know, for she was a first-class gossip. Anna never told her a thing that she did not want repeated, she had learnt that lesson in her first week.

'Two old ladies have bought it, Doctor,' said Miss Willis, 'one is a retired sculptor, the other lady has not said who she is, or what she does, but she would be getting on, I understand.'

'You are losing your skill!' Anna told her, and she laughed. 'You ought to know a great deal more than that about them. Whatever happened to you?'

Miss Willis had unfortunately been out shopping when the lady had gone over the house with the agent, so she had not seen her, but she understood that she lived with a lady friend who had a title, and that they kept three servants and would be moving in fairly soon. The doctors had left the house rather shabby, but nice wallpapers and a fresh coat of paint would make all the difference. Apparently they were going to move in first and do the decorating later on.

Anna thought that they sounded quite pleasant neighbours to have, and she did not ask more.

She had a telephone message from Robin Grant that evening, when she had just finished evening surgery. The play was ending this week. He was extremely worried about it, but he had managed to get another job. A new play was coming on, and he was going to play the lead.

'Much more my cup of tea,' he told her.

The reviews had been horrible, and the house half empty in consequence, and all he hoped was that the world would forget that he had ever been connected with it. A flop of this kind did no actor any good. But he was in love with the new play; he had read the script, which was ideal for him, and the sooner the rehearsals started, the better for him.

To Anna it seemed that this crash had come at the wrong moment. She had disliked the play very much, but had not dared to say so lest it discouraged him. He, for his part, had admitted that it was a pretty poor show, but he had gone on struggling with it, as every good actor does.

She was deeply sorry for him, after all that work, which she knew was terribly tiring, and now in the end it would not have run three weeks. But, as he told her, this was all part of the game.

She had enjoyed seeing Hugh Felton today, he was one of those men who are always the same, and it was a joy that the operation had been such a success. Her home was full of his flowers, and in the larder Miss Willis had lettuces, a cucumber, fresh peas and some broad beans he had given her. He was a wildly generous man, his regret being that he had not sufficient money with which to be really generous.

There was a bug going round at this time. One of those curious start-with-a-headache-and-end-with-vomiting turns which come suddenly, and disappear just as quickly, but it kept her fairly busy.

During this time the people moved in next door. Miss Willis knew all about them, of course, but was worried that they were not encouraging. They had met busybodies before! Anna said 'Good day' to them, but she did not see them very much, for the wretched bug that was going the rounds was taking up a lot of her time.

Then suddenly they sent for her. Would she come over fairly soon, the maid said, for there had been a very nasty accident?

She went immediately.

The house was very pleasant, with new paper on the walls. Now also there were rather extravagant carpets everywhere, deep red, a very comforting colour, and some quite lovely furniture. Before, the floors had been bare with an occasional rug, but this carpeting gave a cheerful warmth to the place.

She went into the big back reception-room, to find that it was now furnished as a drawing-room, with very beautiful furniture, and a grand piano across the far corner, with a huge bowl of red roses standing on it. She would hardly have recognized it.

It was Lady Frey who welcomed her, a tall woman, who walked with an ebony stick, on which she leant heavily. Obviously she had something wrong with her right leg, but she was gracious (had once been very beautiful), and was the sort of woman on whom one could rely.

'I was so sorry to hurry you, Doctor,' she said, 'but my friend, Miss Ambrose, had a fall last night, and hurt her hip; she said it was nothing and went to bed, but today she can't get up.'

'I'll go up and see her,' Anna said.

'She is in pain, and has been most of the night, I am sure, but she never admits to this sort of thing. Will you forgive me for not showing you up, but as you can see I am lame myself,' and she rang for a maid.

Anna went up the wide staircase which had had the cheapest rather nasty carpeting when the old doctors were here, and now had another of those heavy warmly red carpets, into which the footsteps sink, and there is no noise. She was shown into a large back bedroom, well furnished, and went over to the patient lying in the bed.

'I am Dr Thorpe from next door,' she said, 'and I have come to help you. Let me see what is the matter?'

Miss Ambrose was a small woman, rocking herself to and fro with the pain. Very gently Anna laid her back on the pillows. She knew at once that she had wrenched a muscle. She unclipped her bag and got out bandages.

She said, 'I will ease this pain for you in a few minutes, but the bandaging may be a bit uncomfortable. I will try not to hurt you more than I can help, but I have got to get it right.'

She had never had a braver patient than Miss Ambrose, who must have been in very great pain indeed, but was extremely courageous.

'You should have sent for me before,' Anna told her. 'I will always come along at any time, do remember that.'

'But I should have woken you up.'

'Never let that worry you. I am used to that, and I am here to help, and could have eased this wretched pain hours back. It is a shame that you have suffered so much.'

Anna gave her something to help her sleep, and when she had bandaged her, instantly Miss Ambrose felt relief. Anna went downstairs to Lady Frey, who was considerably worried.

She said, 'Poor darling, she never has any luck. If she can hurt herself, she does. It happens like that to some people. Things always turn up at her door, and she does suffer so much with them. She is showing a statue at a big exhibition at Burlington House the week after next, and is worried lest she won't get there.'

Privately Anna thought that it was extremely unlikely that her patient would get there, but not for the world would she depress them more. For the moment she must not get up. Rest was the answer, and she would look in again tonight to see how she was getting on.

She was pleased to have met the people next door, and to have found them so nice, and the big house looked so lovely that it had been a joy to visit it. She went through her work for the morning, then looked at the list of her rounds. It had been a very long surgery, for lately her list of patients had been growing all the time, in spite of the return of the two doctors who really mattered in the place.

It was a busy day, and again another big surgery at night. Then she rang the house next door and asked how the patient was doing.

Lady Frey told her that Miss Ambrose was much more herself and, although there was some pain, it was not too bad. But she was very hungry and was now having her dinner.

'I think I'll pop in to see her,' Anna said, and then, when Lady Frey tried to stop her, 'Oh no, it isn't a trouble, and I want to make sure that she is all right.'

She went up to the bedroom, to find her patient much better; what she had done for her had helped a great deal. She was eating a good dinner, and talking about getting up to 'try out' the leg. Anna hurriedly put a stop to that one!

'Nothing of that sort yet, *please*,' she begged.

'But I want to get to London the week after next.'

'Yes, well, we'll practise for that later,' Anna said.

She did not change the bandages, for she felt that they would be much better as they were, and she again gave her something to help her sleep. 'Rest and quiet are the two best doctors in the whole world,' she told her patient as she went out of the room, and she had a drug which would keep at least the worst of the pain at bay.

During the evening Robin Grant rang her up again from London. He was now exceedingly happy about how the rehearsals for the new play were getting on, and he thought that it should make up for the rotten failure that the last one had been. For the moment they were rushing the rehearsals, because the theatre which they had booked for the play had become vacant sooner than they had anticipated. These were heavy weeks of continuous work, getting word perfect with the script and rehearsing all the time. He added that whatever happened she simply must come up to London for the first night. It could not possibly be the same without her.

While she was sitting there quietly reading the newspaper, she suddenly remembered that she had heard nothing of Dr Graves for three days. By now surely he had got over his wife's death, for he had been expecting it for about three months, but she realized that one's own troubles were always different from those of a patient. She really felt deeply sorry for him.

She knew that he had fretted a great deal, for the last parting is always very hard to bear. His wife had died, and somehow it seems that when this happens one reproaches oneself for things one said or did not say, did or did not do; memory can be very intolerant, and most cruel. It is so easy to blame the past, so difficult to recover from the shock of the great change which comes to all of us.

She had the feeling that something was really wrong, for, after all, his wife had run off with somebody else; he had expected her to die when he knew the disease from which she was suffering; and because, quite suddenly, Anna was worried for him, she rang up his housekeeper and asked if there was anything she could do.

The woman answered the phone in a quite ordinary manner, and then she dropped her voice, which meant that the doctor might be within earshot, and she hesitated slightly, as though she felt that she was disclosing something about which she should keep quiet. Then in a half whisper she said that the doctor had not been well. He was going up to London tomorrow morning to see a surgeon there, for a consultation. She said it with some apprehension.

'Going up to London tomorrow?' Anna asked. 'But why? Is he really ill? Has something gone wrong?' and then quickly, 'I'm his friend.'

'Yes, Doctor, I know, and I am so distressed about him, but he don't like it being talked about.' It was quite obvious that she really was distressed, and that she wanted to confide in Anna. She said that she did not know what was the matter, but the loss of his wife had upset him most dreadfully, and he could not get over it. Once she started to talk, nothing on earth would stop her. He had been seriously agitated about his own health recently, he had lost weight (she put it down to fretting), and now he was going up to London to see about it. But whatever happened Anna must never admit that his housekeeper had given him away.

'Of course not! I do understand and am worried for him, for I never thought that there was anything wrong.'

It was clear that the amiable housekeeper was really scared about him, and Anna said quickly that she would see that not a word of this got out. She added, 'Don't tell the doctor that I rang up, but a little later I'll come round and see him. He may need some help. I'll just drop in.'

The woman answered eagerly, 'Oh, that would be good of you, Doctor. He'd be angry if he knew that I'd said anything, and I am so anxious about him.'

'Of course.'

Anna waited for an hour and a half, and when she rang again the doctor himself answered the phone. She knew by his tone of voice that he was depressed, and he admitted that he had not been feeling at all well, and said he was going up to London tomorrow to see a specialist, because he could not go on doctoring himself and getting nowhere. Of course one was one's own worst doctor, and he managed a little laugh.

She recognized that he was really ill, and he sounded most uneasy. She wondered if she could help in any way. He said he had a small tumour (and that was vague enough), nothing much, and probably of no urgency, but it was no use letting it go on and worry him, so he was going to get a specialist's advice about it.

He knew that he had been overworking ever since he had come back from the war, and probably he had needed time off and a rest, but somehow for the sake of his patients he could not take it. It had not been a very healthy year so far, and every doctor was overworked. There was nothing new in that.

He talked lightly, trying not to disclose the fact that under it all he was frightened, and she said, 'I suppose every one of us gets the odd lump and thinks the worst of it, at some time or other. Half of them are entirely harmless, as we both know,' and she spoke casually. 'Would you like me to come over and have a talk?'

She asked it on the spur of the moment.

'Oh, that would be wonderful,' he replied.

She got a coat and went out of the house, across the street, walking past the three old black and white houses on the far side, leaning over the pavement in the way old shepherds lean when they carry newly-born lambs back from the fields in the spring. She remembered them from her youth. She turned down the side street and rang the shining brass bell in which the housekeeper took such pride. It was the woman herself who answered it, and when she saw who the visitor was, she smiled with the glow of a young girl, yet she could easily have been fifty.

'Oh, it's you, Doctor!' she said, 'I'm ever so glad you've come, for a nice talk is what he wants, and seeing you will cheer him up.'

It was a spacious house, and she went across to the domestic side of it. He was sitting in the dining-room, doing something with an account book, reckoning up visits, she supposed, and when he saw her his whole face was irradicated with a welcome.

'It is so very nice to see somebody,' he said. 'I was wondering how I should kill the time this evening. Doing accounts is rather a poor way, but they have to be done. Seeing you here is a great deal better.'

'I thought perhaps a friendly visit might be helpful. It is always upsetting going to see a specialist, I should hate it myself, because one always expects the worst and gets shattered by one's suspicions.'

He brought out a drink, and they sat down together. He said it was not his lucky year, and he had found in his own life that he had lucky and unlucky years. He had thought that when the 'war to end wars' finished he would come back home and everything would go well.

She said, 'I know, but bad luck does not last for ever. There may be a spot of good luck round the next corner. You never know. You don't look to me like a dying man!'

She thought he was a little quiet, and he commented that disease *was* disease; he had thought that he was well accustomed to it, working with it most of his life, but now suddenly it had distressed him, and in a way that he had never suspected. He had come out of the war with the MC, and the feeling that he had done a good job, and had just got over the fact that his wife had left him. Then she had written a piteous letter while in real trouble in the States, and he blamed himself because he had not been able to help her. It is always so easy to blame oneself. Then she had suddenly died. It had hurt him, for he reproached himself for their marriage going wrong, though it had not really been his fault, and Anna knew it.

'One always blames oneself,' she said.

'And now . . . what?'

She looked at him. She said, 'You think the worst, and are now consulting an important surgeon. I am sure it will be all right, but that won't convince you. I realize that. Now try to appreciate the fact that although all of us must die some day, you and I are not dying at the moment.'

Somehow those words impressed him.

He talked of his wife. They had fallen in love at first sight, when he was on holiday near Innsbrück, doing a walking tour through the mountains. It had been delightful. They had met, two English people walking through the fields rosy with campions flowering everywhere. She had come over to see the Passion Play at Oberammergau, and they had dined together that night and talked of it. He had been there for only ten days and of course all the tickets were sold, so one couldn't get in, or he would have gone with her to see it.

Before he really knew what was happening, they were in love. It had not been passionate love, but a deep affection which both of them felt would be abiding. She was pretty, clever, and sophisticated, and he had never been in love before.

As far as he was concerned, their marriage had been very happy; ultimately they had come to Weston. Then she had met the man with whom she had fallen desperately in love. He had no idea how it had ever happened, and for a time could not believe it was true.

He had hoped that it was one of those passing affairs which come and go, but it was not like that. He believed that perhaps the small country town was not the place for her, for although she had been quite content at first, she had got sick of what she called 'all those old cats who chatter'. It was a good practice and he could not afford to throw it up and go somewhere else. He loved the house, liked the people, and wanted to stay.

In the end she asked for a divorce, and because he still loved her he had given it to her, and she had married the man. She had gone off to the States, and left him to manage as best he could, and for a time he had been very deeply unhappy.

'I oughtn't to be telling you all this,' he said suddenly.

'I don't see why not. I can hold my tongue, as you know, and it will help you to talk about it,' she told him.

His wife had gone off into the blue, in the end behaving most ungraciously, and this had saddened him more than he could stand, and how the small town had talked! Weston lived on other people's troubles, he supposed, it was their way of life, but it had hurt him. He had been almost glad when the war came and he joined up, to get away from it all, and it *had* been a help to him.

'But there are some things that a man can never forget,' she said, realizing that he was very down, and she made him have a really good drink. He became happier on that, less anxious about the wife who had left him and now had died, and less apprehensive about the interview with the specialist tomorrow.

'It is very hard to be a doctor,' she said, 'because we know too much; a specialist can hide things from the ordinary patient, but we see through the little ruses. We know all the tricks, and although we manage to screen our own patients from them, there is always the horror that we cannot screen ourselves.'

She stayed on late with him, talking to him, knowing that the homeliness of simple chat would positively help him far more than anything else. When she left him he was in a much happier mood, and even managed a laugh. He had talked of his boyhood, his early training at St Mary's Hospital, his work there, and his love of it. She went home and was hardly inside the gate before Miss Willis came rushing out to say she was wanted on the phone.

This is a hard life, she thought.

Next day was busy with a lot of calls to make, nothing very serious, but flying from one place to another, and it was the time of year when the narrow country roads were always full. At midday when she returned for an early lunch, for she was operating at the hospital at two, Miss Willis told her that Robin Grant had rung up, and would ring again when she was having her lunch. 'Now what does he want?' she asked herself. The new play was coming on next week, she had already read notes about it in the newspaper, and had tucked a little reminder on to her engagement book for the day and the fact that she must send him a telegram of good wishes.

He rang up just as she sat down to her lunch. He wanted her to come up to the first night, if only to bring him luck.

'I didn't bring you much luck last time, with the show off in three weeks,' she reminded him.

He said, 'You helped me no end, although you didn't know it, and if that show did not put you off too much, do please come to this one. I can book a room for you at the same hotel and we will do exactly as we did before.'

It so happened that they were very busy at the moment, in the summer there always seemed to be much more to do, and she felt that she could not possibly get away at such short notice. Instantly he seemed to be appalled.

Apparently he had been sure within himself that she would be certain to come, almost as though it were a steady arrangement between themselves, and he had even troubled to check it with the hotel. 'I've been up to the neck in frantic rehearsals, and this play is quite something, I can promise you that; somehow I never thought of asking you, because I felt that it was the accepted thing; I have a first night, and you come to it.'

Gently she said that this was very short notice. One could not just walk out of a practice like this. One had to make arrangements in advance for somebody to carry on in one's absence, and the man who had carried on for her last time happened to be ill, he was in fact in London seeing a specialist today; she could hardly bother him again.

She knew by his tone of voice that he was horrified.

'I want to see you here so much. You don't seem to appreciate how I feel about it. I always think that you bring me luck.'

'I certainly didn't last time!' she reminded him again.

'It was my own fault getting myself involved in such a deadly play. I was talked into it, and that is always a mistake. I ought to have known that the damned thing would never work out, and of course it didn't. You simply must come up to this one. *Please?*'

It was then that she knew that it would be the wrong thing to do. In life it is always hard to see the right path to tread, the road along which one should walk, when there are so many temptations to veer to the right or the left. But she had her job here. This invitation had come at a time when she just could not accept it, and she was speaking the truth when she said that they were very busy and she could not come.

'I am so sorry, truly sorry, but I can't do it. I will wish you all the luck in the world, and in spirit I shall be with you.' In life it is always strange how suddenly one comes to the turning point in the path along which one is walking, and finds that one makes new decisions, dreams new dreams, and the whole of our outlook changes. She said, 'As I said, one of our doctors is ill, it may very easily be quite serious, and he needs help. It would be unwise for me to go away at the moment.'

'I do need you.'

'And I should love to come and give you all the support in the world, but I have my job to do, and at this moment it would be so very awkward to leave it.'

She knew that he desperately wanted her there and she was sorry to disappoint him, but her work here had to come first at whatever the cost. She soothed him down and wished him luck, then had a quick snack and flew off to the hospital theatre to operate. She was expecting Dr Graves home today, and was very worried, for she had received no message from him. She had rather thought that if all was well he would have rung her up, but he had not done so. She went off to the theatre, and perhaps because she was worried that she had disappointed Robin Grant, as she knew she had, and that she had not heard from Dr Graves, things did not go as smoothly as usual. Inwardly she knew that she was torn two ways. Afterwards she made three or four visits, and then took her surgery. Just as it was ending, the telephone rang, and when she picked up the receiver, she heard Dr Graves's voice at the other end.

'Dr Graves speaking. Is that Anna?' and then quickly, 'Don't worry about me, I've had a marvellous day, and the whole thing is nothing at all, a mere trifle.' He went into technical details, rushing through the words with a thrill in his excited voice. Then he said, 'Do come round here and see me. I'm only having a cold supper, and I could tell you all about it from A to Z. I can hardly believe my luck'—he laughed as he said it—'and I am just all of a glow.'

She went along to sup with him, and he himself opened the door to her. She thought that he looked years younger. A doctor's life is working all the time fighting illness and death, hideous diseases which creep up quietly and bring with them the darkness of the grave itself, but for the moment Dr Graves had forgotten all about that.

He said, 'I thought the war asked enough of one, never getting a full night's sleep, being eternally on the go, and for ever playing with death. That sort of strain takes it out of one more than one appreciates at the time. One finds it out later on. And it seems to be the same with a private practice.'

She suggested a holiday, even if it was only a long weekend, as the chance to get an undisturbed night's rest, would be a help.

They sat down to their homely supper together. It was a relief to get away from her own telephone.

He was extremely cheerful over the delightful meal. He was one of those doctors who worry themselves too much over their patients. And like most doctors, he was always anxious for his own health. But now, she told him, life had changed and he had a new life ahead. He was talking very gaily, and she realized that companionship helped him, and she herself was very happy that his present trouble was at an end.

They talked of the little country town. People thought that nothing ever happened in the country, yet things were happening all the time. But he was glad to be back here.

'It's quiet, and that means a lot to a man who has served in a war,' he said.

'It's restful after a fashion, as restful as any doctor's life can be.'

He was trying to plan a holiday abroad, though he did not think that he was really entitled to this. She thought that it would be a very good idea.

'You ought to have a taste of having nothing to do,' she suggested.

'It is not so easy for a doctor to go off into the blue taking holidays,' he told her. 'I was away long enough in that infernal war.'

She changed the subject and told him of Robin's play coming on soon, and how she had refused to go up to London. He said that he thought she had done the wrong thing in not accepting his invitation. 'Surely you realize that he wants you there? He thinks you bring him luck.'

'He can't possibly imagine that seeing what happened last time!'

'I still think that you ought to go. One is only young once and there are so many happy things to do whilst one is young, and these fade out as one gets older. I can act for you; after all, that is fair do's, you have helped me whilst I was away, and it would do you good.'

'I can't go.'

'But why ever not? He thinks that you can help him, and he must be strung up to a fairly high pitch, for it is very nerve-racking to be waiting to come on for the first night of a new play. One must understand that he needs help.'

She paused before answering. 'It is a bit late in the day to change my mind now,' she said.

'Why? I've come back fit and well, nothing to worry about, and I am quite prepared to help you.'

She felt herself filled with a sudden flood of real excitement. She had never thought that she wanted to go so much.

'Phone him now and tell him that you are going to come after all.'

She demurred for a moment, then suddenly she thought that perhaps he was right, that she should make the effort to go, and that it would help Robin. The last time she had gone to see his play she had appreciated the terrific strain it entailed, and the effort.

When she rang up, he was not at home, for there was another late rehearsal. 'My goodness, they do work these actors!' she told herself as she got the woman who ran his flat for him. Would she tell him that after all she had changed her mind and would like to come up to the first night of his new play, and wish him luck? The woman sounded very glad that she was doing this.

She said, 'He has the idea that you bring him luck. He is getting awfully tired with all the rehearsals they are having, and this will buck him up. I'll tell him the minute he gets in.'

She rang off and turned to the doctor. 'Your advice was good, you told me the right thing,' she said.

CHAPTER ELEVEN

Robin was enchanted when he heard; he rang up saying now he knew that the play would be a success, and he would re-book her a room at the hotel and they would dine out after the show. He would make all the arrangements.

She had not wanted to go to this first night, but he had set so much store by it, and somehow Dr Graves had talked her into it. Robin had been the first real friend she had met since that gruelling winter when she had been settling down into the practice, and she owed him that much. Possibly when she had walked on the downs she had been in the mood for love, she told herself, possibly she had worked too hard, and maybe he was right in getting her up to London.

On the appointed day she caught the early train. She had bought a little silk dress in which to travel, and an evening dress which would be entirely useless to her in Weston, but she had to have it. She went straight to the same hotel, and had a rest, for the journey had been hot and stuffy and it had tired her. She had been called out twice during the previous night, and now she had a deep sleep, which surprised her. There was perhaps something in getting away from the telephone.

She dressed in good time, pleased with the frock she had bought, and when she got to the theatre, crowded out, the usherette said, 'Dr Thorpe, isn't it?' and she gave her a spray of green orchids to go with her dress. She remembered that Robin had asked the colour of her dress. Perhaps she knew then that she had reached a crossroads in her life.

'Now I can relax,' she told herself.

The orchestra started up and there came the great moment when the theatre darkened and the curtain rolled up. The hour had come!

As the play went on Anna realized that Robin was making the very most of his part, and doing it magnificently. That man *could* act. She was very much impressed, and when the curtain fell on the last act, the audience became wildly enthusiastic. They cheered, and there was no doubt about this being a success, as all the world could see. She went round to his dressing-room, and everybody seemed to be there. In the end he got rid of them with some difficulty, changed, then threaded an arm through hers, and they went to the stage door together. When they got to the restaurant, he was instantly recognized; undoubtedly he had done extraordinarily well. But it had taken it out of him, and he was tired.

He said, 'All I want is food. I haven't been able to eat all day; nerves, I suppose,' and he gave a grin.

He ordered a good meal, and they sat down in a quiet corner which he had reserved for himself and her, a little screened off from the crowd, because he had realized he would be recognized after the play's success.

'It has worn me out,' he said.

'I'm sure it must have. It is one of those professions which ask everything of you, like mine. Only you don't get called out at night!'

'I couldn't stick that,' he said.

'It's part of the job, and until I met you I never knew how much your job would ask of you.'

'It's those awful rehearsals. The producer was not satisfied and would run through the second act again this afternoon. It terrified me that it would wear us all out, but we did it, and I realize now that it was the right thing to do. I was specially worried, having had that failure this year. No actor can afford a couple of them, and this one had to be *it*. I admit it took a lot out of me.'

'Yes, of course,' and she said it very gently. 'Until I met you I always thought acting was one of what I called the playboy professions. Now I know what darned hard work it can entail. Anyway, tonight was a tremendous success.'

They lingered over the meal, he feeling relaxed, and she knew that he was a great deal more content. He realized that there would be a good press in the morning. Then he started to talk about her.

'Do you intend to stay on where you are?'

'Of course! I put up my plate, and that is that!'

'I thought it was the wrong thing to do?'

'Yes, it was, but I just couldn't help myself.'

He said, 'You'll get tired of it as life goes on. You ought to marry and have someone to see after you, and keep you, too.'

She shook her head. 'I did not train to be a doctor with the idea of not staying in the profession. I wanted a country practice. Harley Street would not be my line, for I want to know my patients. They are my friends, and that is what I want, too.'

'But surely to goodness you can't waste your whole life in that little town?'

She smiled at that. 'It is *not* a waste. I now have a host of friends. Harley Street is just a passageway through which a crowd of strangers pass.'

She thought of the river rippling through the town, and the spire of the church cut clear against the sky, so lovely at sunset. She added, 'It takes all sorts to make a world, you know.'

He was silent for a moment, playing with a glass, twisting it round and round; the waiter came and went, almost like a shadow, without a sound, and then Robin blurted out his thoughts. 'I want to marry you,' he said.

Perhaps she had not realized that all the time she had known that this was in the background of their lives, but somehow had thrust it aside. Now suddenly she came face to face with the problem. She knew that she *was* standing at the crossways of her own life, and for a single second she did not know what to say or do. In that moment she thought of Richard Graves, the doctor at Weston. She considered the question, then she began to speak very quietly.

'I am not sure that I want to marry,' she said. 'When I went to the island at Easter I was tired and was in need of a holiday, a complete change from Weston, somewhere right away from everything I knew and was doing. It *was* a big change for me, I had not had a holiday for years, spending all my life studying and taking the degrees I wanted, working in hospital, and working really hard! Then, when I had put up my plate, it meant simply driving at it, day and night, getting settled in, which I did. I suppose I was lucky as the war was still on, and so I got the opportunity to establish myself before the two good men came home. The competition was fairly poor in Weston. But it did entail tremendously hard work.'

'And you ought to give it up.' He said it with confidence, and she wondered that a man so fond of his own profession could speak that way of someone else's job. Maybe we all see it from another angle, maybe we do not understand.

'I doubt if I *could* give it up,' she told him.

'Marry me, and live happily ever after?'

It was at that moment, in the gay, highly modern restaurant, with good food and wine, and an orchestra playing softly in the distance, that she knew she could not possibly do it. The long years of training and the triumph of helping someone else in pain, even saving him from death itself, meant too much for her to abandon it.

She said, 'I wanted to be a doctor. It is my life, and I chose it. It means very much to me.'

For a moment he did not believe that he had heard aright. Then he said, 'You're joking!' and stopped dead, with a glass half-way to his lips.

'No, I am not. I am happy there. It is something to feel that one is wanted, and I never discovered how much I valued it until now. The people need me, and I couldn't fail them.' She spoke quite calmly.

He argued, of course. All along she must have known that he was in love with her and wanted to marry her, and now, just when he had had the biggest success of his life, she was actually refusing him. He had had a great reception tonight, his future was made, but what he asked was impossible.

She shook her head, and now she knew that what she said was the truth. 'I'm so delighted that you had this triumph tonight, for another failure would have been the end. Your work means a great deal to you, as mine means to me. I am doing what I believe to be right. I want to continue being a doctor. I want to get people out of pain, and save their lives. I don't want to marry and then settle down.'

He stared at her, utterly dismayed. Almost as if he could not believe what she had said. She recognized the fact that she had never been so positive to him before.

When he spoke again his voice was tense. 'When we met that day on the island, I fell in love with you at first sight. I daresay you think this is a lot of nonsense, but it happens to be quite true. I know what your work asks of you and what a strain it must be, but I want to help you. I want to have you with me all my life.'

She said, 'I do know that. Don't think that I do not understand, for I do.' He had come into her life at the time when she was tired and worried and needed a friend, but she had never thought of marriage. She went on. 'Both of us have our lives before us, and for the moment I don't want to make any immediate change in mine.'

She was not sure that, as a doctor, she could live in London and practise with an actor husband going and coming, experiencing all the tension of arduous rehearsals, the glow or the collapse of first nights, and the reaction which all this would entail. She loved him in her own way, but she was not in love, and that is a very different story. She admired his art, she liked his characteristics, but to be his wife would mean that the stress would be too much for her. For one moment she asked herself, was she in love with her work and putting it before everything else? In a way she wanted to love Robin Grant, and yet to be herself. Perhaps all losers face these problems at some time.

She had worked herself to death to prove to her patients that she was the doctor who would come round whenever she was called, and would do her best. She had been astonishingly successful in the small town, probably because—the good men being away—the patients were in the hands of old-fashioned lackadaisical doctors who were too old to bother too much.

Weston had liked her from the first. She *had* had a lot of luck in addition to the hard work. Life was for ever offering or removing opportunities. But now, if she faced the truth, she would know that her heart was unsure of itself. Robin was enchanting, devoted to his job as she was to hers. But she had made up her mind that she could never desert the people who wanted her. A hard job, but very very rewarding.

She told him, 'I love my job, and I don't think I could give it up. And it would be wrong to waste all that training, from which other people want to benefit, and do nothing.'

He said protestingly, 'But I love you, and *I* want *you*.'

She said, 'I know. But life is going to change a lot, and this is no time to be thinking of ourselves. The whole world will change.'

'But think of our own future in that world. I hope things will eventually settle down, though I can't be too sure.'

She said in a low voice, 'Nor can I. We have fought a desperate war, and a great deal of power has gone to the wrong people. I feel that now we might have to fight the peace.'

He stared at her as though he did not understand what she said, and after a minute she spoke again. Sitting here in a corner of the great restaurant, talking of their own futures and what lay ahead of them, she realized that perhaps after all she had come to a turning point in her life. There are moments when one is aware of this, moments when one sees the future beckoning, almost hears a voice calling.

'It is great to have peace,' she went on, 'great to have a future.'

He nodded. 'Yes. It was a hard war, and we have earned the peace. And we both work hard in our jobs, night and day. I worked extra hard this time, for that last play worried me. It was the first real failure I have had since I got to stardom, and nobody likes that sort of thing. But now I have come round the corner. Tonight *was* a success, and it should wipe out the impact of the other.'

'People's memories are short-lived.'

'Yes, I know,' and then he paused. 'I do wish you felt differently about your job. It is far too heavy work for any woman to do, day and night, night and day, if you ask me, and no let-up of any sort.'

'But you put in long hours at rehearsals, and so do the actresses. We all have to work hard if we are to do anything and get anywhere, surely you realize that?'

Again he paused a moment, twiddling the wine glass in an uneasy way, probably not even aware of what he was doing. He said, 'But our work is different.'

She told him, 'My work matters, too, you know. Don't forget that.'

'Yes, but so does mine.' He began to recall how he had broken into the acting world, in the late teens. His people had been against it, but he had got a tiny part in a London show, and then as an understudy, and from that he had never looked back. At first he had eaten the most frugal meals because he was out of work, and was terrified that he would never get another job. But the war had helped him. He had a dicky heart and could not join up. He said that the heart would never kill him (when he told her about it she knew that immediately), and the fact that so many of the good men joined up meant that he had got better parts.

'All luck,' he said, 'and if you ask me luck is the key to the door every time. Now I want us to marry and live happily ever after.'

'I've told you, there *is* my practice.'

'You can't marry your practice, you know.'

She told him then how hard the last months had been, a steady drive to establish herself, for the two old boys next door had done everything they could to upset her, and she knew they had spoken against her, and had tried to put patients off her. But she *was* young, she *was* new, and she did come when called. 'That was the answer,' she told him with a laugh.

They had drunk champagne, it was that sort of a night. Later he drove her back to the hotel, and kissed her good night. They had got no further with any future plans, but she had known that they never would. Her work meant too much to her. It was her life companion, walking quietly beside her. She went into the hotel with the lovely orchids pinned to her dress, and the feeling that she had today passed another milestone in her life. There was a message for her from her home, a telephone message. It seemed that Lady Porth was none too well. Anna phoned through even though it was past midnight already. It was Lord Porth who spoke to her. His wife was asleep now, and had been feeling what she called 'funny' all day. They were very worried when they could not get her.

She said, 'I'll catch the first train down, I'll see about it right now. Don't disturb her.' She only hoped that baby was not getting sick of things and making an unexpected entry into the world. She left an order with the night porter to be called in time to catch the first train.

She had packed before she lay down and she arrived at Paddington station in the very early morning, when it is not one of the most welcoming places in this hard world. There seemed to be an enormous amount of luggage about.

She was very worried for Lady Porth.

It was one of those most unpromising summer days with a faint drizzle, and she had only the lightest coat with her and felt quite cold. The moment she got back to Weston, she went straight home, had a sandwich, and then got the car out and went over to the Porths. In the country the weather was clearing, the hills receding into the distance, which is always a good omen for the future. She turned in at the park gates with the awful premonition that this would go wrong for her. The butler opened the door and told her that Dr Graves had been here already today, and her Ladyship had started to feel ill after he had gone. Lord Porth came out of the library to meet her.

'She was all right until an hour ago,' he said.

'I'll go up and see what I can do for her. No good hanging about. If the baby wants to come now, he will have to.'

As she went up the uncarpeted polished stairs she had the feeling that this was going to be difficult, and was almost glad that it was going to end now. She went into the big bedroom with the glorious view of the park, and the deer browsing there. She always thought that there was something very sweet about deer, they looked so lovely, and added to the scene.

Lady Porth was glad to see her.

'Oh, thank goodness you've come! I've had enough of this,' she said.

The condition was exactly the one that Anna had suspected when she had got the message last night. The baby intended to arrive six weeks before he was expected, and then, she told herself, he will probably be a girl to add to the trouble he has caused. It was half-past two when she brought the child into the world, and thanked heaven that at least he had the decency to be another son. Twenty minutes later when Lady Porth came to, she told her that all was well.

'It's a boy,' she said.

'Oh, I am so glad. My husband was mad on another son, and now he's here. Let me see him.'

Anna took him to her. Not a particularly pretty baby, but which of them is when newly born? she asked herself. She left the patient to the two midwives with her, and went downstairs. Until this moment she had not appreciated the fact that she had had a very early breakfast and no lunch. Now she saw that the butler had thought of this for her, and it was waiting on the table, Lord Porth with it.

He said, 'If you caught the first train, as you did, there is no refreshment car on it, and you must have some sustenance, and drink to my new son. My wife wanted a boy, does she know?'

'She came round a few minutes ago, and I told her at once. She was enchanted.'

'That's good,' said Lord Porth.

Anna sat down to eat a very good lunch, for

which she was grateful, for what the hotel had called an 'early breakfast' was just coffee and toast. She was thankful that this was over and the child was the right sex, alive and definitely kicking, and there should be no fear on his behalf.

He seemed to be sturdy.

But she knew that she was very tired. Lord Porth thanked her again and again, and she did not stay for coffee, she wanted to get home and have a rest before she tackled the evening surgery. She only prayed that there were no calls waiting for her. Before she went, she had a last look at the mother and her baby, both of whom seemed to be very well. Then she went home, and told Miss Willis to stave off any further calls until half past five. Whatever happened, she simply must get some sleep now.

She woke for surgery feeling considerably better. Miss Willis had dealt with all the calls, and said that Dr Graves wanted her to go in tonight after dinner, and she said that she would.

It was one of those lovely summer evenings when the surgery filled up, but the air was close with thunder about, making things rather tiresome.

The surgery was one of the most trying she

had ever had, with two of the good old toughs being extremely difficult. Then she had a rest and her dinner, and went across the road to Dr Graves's house, aware that the rest had done her good, and she felt better. She had phoned for news of Lady Porth, and she and the baby were doing well.

'I have done an awful lot of work since I got back,' she told Richard Graves.

They sat there in the pleasant room backing on to the garden, and the cosiness of the place had charm after the hotel in London. The garden was glorious, he was the most interested gardener himself.

'It is so nice here,' she said, and realized that this was the very moment when the curtain would be rising on Robin's new play.

'How did your friend do?'

'I thought he did very well, and he got a tremendous reception. He wanted a big success, and he got it.' She paused a moment, and then she said, 'I must admit that he acts awfully well.'

The doctor said nothing for a while, then he said, 'I suppose you are not thinking of marrying him?'

She was quite surprised at the question, for somehow she had not thought that he would think of it. 'He is a very good companion, but

I have always thought that his career is not right for a happy marriage. Too many ups and downs. He can never really settle to living life, for there is always another play ahead of him.'

'Yes, of course.'

She said, 'He is the most charming man, and so kind, but his is not the right life for marriage, surely? It means continual change, everlasting uncertainty, and I don't think that after being a doctor I could take it. I shall never hurry into marriage.'

He nodded, then he said, 'I think you are probably right there. But your job ought not to stand between yourself and happiness. I know that a doctor's life is very difficult, for ever on the rounds or operating, but at least he can share a home, in spite of the eternally hard work, but an actor can't, as he is for ever in the theatre or on the move.'

'The whole of stage life is based on insecurity, and to me that is not a very satisfactory idea.' She sighed as she said it.

It was then that, quite calmly, he told her again of his own love story. He had married his wife for love. He had just qualified and had to find a practice immediately and earn money.

She understood that, and she thought

again of walking on Tennyson Downs with Robin, and even then being aware that his job was the ghostly stranger who walked with them. No actor can get rid of his job. She had loved that holiday, it would always stand out as one of the big landmarks in her life.

She said, 'I came here and worked too hard, of course, but all of us have to do that at some time or other. My medicine and his stage work would never fit in together. I know that. He lives on his nerves. I live on cool, calm common sense. We have to.'

He smiled a little as he said, 'You've got something there, it is the background of all doctors' lives,' and then rather quietly, 'I was a little worried that you would marry him.'

'You needn't worry. The two careers cannot fit in, anybody can see that.'

'You will get a very good practice here, and you have worked very hard for it.'

She laughed at that. She was still young enough to take hard work in her stride. 'I'm staying here, I hope,' she said.

He put out a very slender hand, delicately made, a true surgeon's hand, she told herself, and he laid it very tenderly over her own. She felt a sudden urge of joy in her heart. 'I want to do everything that I can to help you,' he said. He had a very beautiful voice, a man who had suffered a great deal, as she knew, but he had been spared the horror of bringing his wife back here to die.

Tenderly she said, 'Life does work out for the best in many ways, though it may be hard to see it at the time. Suffering teaches us how to live.'

'And I really thought you were going to marry that fellow and leave us.'

She said 'No,' very quietly. 'What is more it could not have worked out well. Once a doctor, always a doctor.'

'So you will stay on here, and there will never be another war, that is one mercy. I'm glad you are here, there's room for all of us.'

'I'm glad, too,' she said.

His hand still lay over her own, and at that moment it seemed as if a new world had opened wide its doors, and through the aperture she saw a world that was entirely different, something that she had never dreamed of before.

She did not know how long they sat like that. Then she drew her hand away, and she saw his reproachful eyes.

'You're not going? You'll come back?'

'Of course!' she said.

It was then that she knew the future that

lay ahead of her, it was then that she felt suddenly overjoyed. 'I am so happy,' she said spontaneously.